FRESH STARTS AT FOLLY FARM

Rachel and her son Sam have moved back to the farm where she grew up — now a shadow of its former self, all livestock gone. Then a horse appears in the stables overnight! The culprit is Xander, an actor seeking an anonymous holiday in Bramblewick, who has rescued the horse from his cruel owner. Soon word gets around that Folly Farm is taking in old and unwanted animals, and the menagerie grows — as does the mutual attraction between Rachel and Xander . . .

SHARON BOOTH

FRESH STARTS AT FOLLY FARM

Complete and Unabridged

LINFORD
Leicester

First published in Great Britain in 2018

First Linford Edition
published 2019

A catalogue record for this book is available
from the British Library.

ISBN 978–1–4448–4164–0

Published by
F. A. Thorpe (Publishing)
Anstey, Leicestershire

Set by Words & Graphics Ltd.
Anstey, Leicestershire
Printed and bound in Great Britain by
T. J. International Ltd., Padstow, Cornwall

This book is printed on acid-free paper

1

'There's a horse in our stables.'

Rachel froze, her mug of hot tea held in suspension as she absorbed her mum's words. There was no horse in the stables at Folly Farm; there hadn't been horses at the farm for half a century, so she'd always been told. The last occupant of that stable had been Milkmaid, her ill-tempered and rather flighty pony, whose moods and displays of shockingly bad behaviour had so terrified her when she was a nine-year-old child that her dad had sold her to the father of one of her classmates. She could still remember the shame of being laughed at in school by Susan Rudd, who had informed everyone that Rachel was too feeble to control a timid little pony. Milkmaid had then compounded her humiliation by behaving like an angel for Susan, winning just about every rosette and cup it was possible to earn at various pony club events.

There had been no occupants in the farm's now rather rundown stables since, so the fact that her mother was suddenly convinced they housed a horse was deeply worrying. Was this, she wondered, the start of it? Obviously, her mother was getting older, but surely seventy-two was still young these days? But then, Rachel had sensed a depression in her mum that she'd tried to talk to her about, only to be firmly shut down with the scathing words, 'Nothing wrong with me, love. Stop mithering.'

She should have been firmer, she thought, placing the mug on the kitchen table and closing her eyes briefly. She would have to make her an appointment at the surgery. There was no evidence of dementia, but depression could have a strange effect on the mind, and her mum was so listless lately. So lacking in enthusiasm. So totally different to the way she'd always been. She would need assessing, maybe referring . . . It was all too much, she thought despairingly.

She took a deep breath and yelled at the top of her voice, 'Sam! Are you nearly ready? Come on, you're going to be late!'

'Are you even listening to me?' Her mum sounded excited, almost like her old self. Rachel knew she missed having animals on the farm. Maybe she was hallucinating because she so wanted it to be true. It would be a cow tomorrow, or a sheep. She'd better have a word with Connor or Riley. They would know what to do.

'I said,' her mum continued, 'there's a horse in our stables. Heard clattering in there, so I opened the top door of the loose box, and there he was. Come and have a look at him.'

Rachel considered this dilemma. She knew it was better to go along with a person's delusion, rather than try to argue with them. If she told her mum she was imagining it, she knew only too well that she would get annoyed and defiant. Her mum would argue black was white rather than admit she was mistaken. On the other hand, if she accompanied her to the stables, what should she do then? Stand and stare at an empty space, and agree with her mother that the horse was a fine specimen, and maybe they should find him a carrot?

She took a gulp of her tea to buy her some time, realising too late that it was still very hot. Too hot. She gasped out loud and slammed the mug down on the table again.

Her mother didn't appear to notice that her daughter had scalded the roof of her mouth. 'Come on, see what you think.'

Rachel headed to the sink, poured herself a cup of cold water, and swilled the liquid around in her mouth. 'Think about what, Mum?' she said, finally resigning herself to the fact that she wasn't going to get away with this. Her mother was going to make her go to the stables, and she was going to have to deal with the problem when she got there.

'What's up with you?' Her mum's eyes narrowed, and she stared at Rachel curiously. 'I've just told you there's a horse in our stables, and you're not showing the slightest bit of interest. Don't you want to know where it came from? 'Cause I'm sure I do.'

Rachel smiled encouragingly at her. 'Come on, then. Let's go and see this horse of yours.'

Her mother scowled. 'It's no horse of mine, is it? Not had horses here for years.' She gave a little chuckle. 'Remember that little grey pony of yours? By heck, your dad always said she ran rings around you.'

Trust her to remember that! 'Sam! I won't tell you again!'

There was a muffled thud from upstairs and a resentful voice called, 'I'm nearly ready. Just *wait* a minute.'

Rachel rolled her eyes, took her

mum's hand, and together they headed out into the yard. As if she wasn't stressed enough already, what with a house that was falling to bits around her ears, a new job to get used to, and a seven-year-old son already struggling to understand the changes in his life, who was now faced with starting over in a new school where he knew no one. She'd known her mum wasn't quite right — it was, in truth, the main reason she'd taken the job in Bramblewick — but this listlessness and overwhelming *sadness* was scary. No doubt about it. She would have to talk to one of the GPs, and —

'There's a horse in our stables.'

She couldn't quite believe it, and wondered for a moment if she was imagining things too. She shouldn't be surprised if she was, what with the stress she was under. But no. As she peered closer, she realised the horse was very real indeed. He was a big, hairy cob, and he was staring at her over the loose box door with large, dark eyes, half-hidden under a thick forelock that was as long as Dumbledore's beard.

'Never! Is there really?' Her mother's voice was heavy with sarcasm, and Rachel felt a sudden relief that she wasn't imagining things after all. The horse was real! Thank goodness! Then she frowned. The horse was real. So who had put a great big lump of a horse in their stables?

'Poor thing looks proper grubby,' her mum said thoughtfully. 'Needs grooming. I wonder if I can find some of our old grooming equipment in the tack room? Might have a few — '

'Don't you dare!' Rachel's voice was sharper than she intended, and she softened it as she continued. 'He could be dangerous, Mum. A biter or a kicker. And I don't want you going in that stable while I'm not here, either, do you hear me?'

Ignoring her, her mother headed straight for the loose box door and un-bolted the bottom half. 'He's knocked his bucket of water over. I'd better fill that up for him.'

She reached out and stroked the muzzle of the chestnut cob; who, thankfully, showed no inclination to rear up and assert his authority over this strange woman. Rachel held her breath, but relaxed a little as the horse lowered his head and gently nudged her mother with what almost seemed like affection.

'Okay, Mum, that's enough. Come out of there now. I've got to get to work.' She glanced at her watch and her face paled. 'I'm going to be late.'

'You get off, then,' her mum said comfortably. 'I'll be right as rain here.'

'You must be joking! There's no way I'm leaving you alone with this huge creature, however friendly he may seem. Anything could happen.'

Her mother tutted. 'Your dad always said you were too scared of horses for your own good. Look, go and fill up this bucket for him, there's a good lass.' She shook her head. 'Could do with some meat on his bones, too, bless him.'

Rachel knew there was no point arguing. Her mum wouldn't shift until the horse was comfortable. She thought about the time and felt a twinge of panic. There was still no sign of Sam. She had to drop him off at the breakfast club at school before heading to the surgery. She would be late, and it was only her third week at work. How was that going to look? She had patients to see. There would be a queue in the waiting room. She could hear the mutterings and complaints now. Connor would call her into his room and lecture her on punctuality. He was a nice man, as was Riley — much nicer than the GPs she'd worked with at her previous job — but even so . . .

She sighed and filled the bucket from the tap in the yard, wishing she'd worn wellies. It had been pouring down with rain all night, and the yard was wet and muddy. She would have to clean the mud off her shoes now, which would delay her even further.

Sam appeared in the yard, his tawny hair ruffled, and his shirt only half-tucked into his school trousers. 'What are you doing out here?' His expression changed when he caught sight of his grandma standing beside a sturdy chestnut cob. 'A horse! Cool! Whose is he?'

'Good question,' Rachel muttered as she lugged the bucket over to the loose box and reluctantly placed it inside.

'He should be outdoors, really,' her mum said thoughtfully. 'This type of horse doesn't need to be cooped up. He's a hardy cob. And he needs food. There's nothing in there for him. If only we had some hay or something. I'll turn him out into the paddock.'

'You'll do no such thing,' Rachel said immediately. 'We don't know who he belongs to. Leave him where he is, and I'll make some enquiries.'

'But if he's in our stable, doesn't that make him ours?' Sam said hopefully.

His grandmother laughed and ruffled his already untidy hair. 'I reckon it does.'

'It so does not,' Rachel said, her

spirits sinking even further when her son shot her a look of resentment. 'We can't keep him, Sam. He must belong to someone.'

'Someone with no scruples about dumping him in a total stranger's stable,' her mum pointed out. 'And look at the state of him! He's proper muddy, and his mane and tail need a good comb-through. Poor lad.' She patted the horse's nose, then stepped back into the yard, bolting the loose box door behind her, to Rachel's relief.

'Can I stay and help Nanna look after him?' Sam queried.

'You have to get to the breakfast club, and I'm already running late. Don't look like that, Sam. You know I have patients waiting. My first appointment's at eight, and it's only your third week at school. You don't want to make a bad impression.'

'As if I care,' he mumbled sulkily, and she bit down an angry retort. She was doing her best, for goodness' sake. What more could she do?

11

Her mother's eyes were full of sympathy. 'You and your mum get off, Sam,' she said to her grandson, squeezing his shoulder. 'I reckon the horse will be still be here when you get home tonight. We'll decide what to do about him then, eh?'

Sam looked eagerly at his nan, and Rachel sighed inwardly. Now he would be convinced that they would be keeping the horse, and of course they couldn't, He wasn't theirs to keep. But the question was, whose was he? And why on earth had he been dumped in the rundown stables of Folly Farm?

2

'We've got a right one in there.' Holly hurried into the office, rudely interrupting the conversation between Rachel and the head receptionist, Anna.

Anna rolled her eyes as Holly nodded her head towards the waiting room. 'Go and have a sneaky peek. Must be a superhero in disguise. Or a complete nutter.'

Rachel bit her lip, trying not to smile. It was hardly professional to discuss a patient in such a fashion, something that Anna clearly recognised, as she was shaking her head despairingly at their colleague.

'For goodness' sake, Holly, how many more times? Don't talk about them like that.'

Holly pulled a face, then winked at Rachel. 'Go and have a look then,' she said lightly, turning to Anna. 'See what you think. Go on, I dare you.'

Anna tutted. 'Certainly not.' Her eyes, however, strayed to the door, and Rachel was pretty sure she was dying to take a sneaky peek. She was far too responsible to do so, though, as it might well encourage Holly. 'Who's he here to see?'

Holly grinned and nodded over to Rachel. 'One of yours. New patient check. Good luck with that.'

Rachel sighed. 'Great. Just what I need.' Then she remembered Anna was watching and switched on a smile. 'I'm sure it will be fine. Anyway,' she added as an afterthought, 'what's so strange about him?'

Holly needed no further encouragement. Grabbing Rachel's arm, she practically dragged her over to the door and hissed in her ear, 'Go on, have a look. The man in black. You can't miss him.'

Rachel peered into the waiting room, trying to look as if she wasn't searching for a specific patient. Her gaze fell on the man hunched in a chair on the back row of the room, and she withdrew quickly, her lips twitching with amusement. 'Well, maybe he's got a headache.'

Anna was checking Rachel's appointment list. 'Alexander South. I was at the desk when he came in to register. Seemed perfectly normal to me.' She shrugged. 'What do you mean, *maybe he's got a headache?*'

'Have a look for yourself if you're so keen to find out,' was Holly's retort. 'Honestly, he looks as if he's about to rob a bank.'

Rachel wanted to laugh, but didn't dare. It was all right for Holly. Although they'd actually started working at the Bramblewick surgery on the same day — Holly as receptionist, and she as practice nurse — Holly had the advantage of being a villager, familiar with the surgery and already a friend of Anna and the two GPs. Rachel, on the other hand, hadn't lived in Bramblewick for many years. When she'd left the village to go to nursing college, old Dr Gray and Dr

Pennington-Rhys had been the GPs. Now Connor Blake, Anna's husband, and Riley MacDonald were the partners. Although she'd really taken to Holly, who was quite forthright and cheerful, Rachel still felt like the new girl — which, to be fair, she was, having only been a member of staff for two weeks, yet Holly had settled in as if she'd worked there for years, which was a bit discouraging.

'Don't be so mean,' Anna said, a definite gleam of amusement in her eyes. 'If we all go to have a look, he'll get suspicious.'

Holly gave an exaggerated smile. 'I suppose so. Well, he's sitting all hunched up, as if he doesn't want anyone to see him, and he's wearing a black woolly hat and a black jacket zipped right up to his bearded chin — '

'Well, it *is* still cold out there,' Anna pointed out. 'You can't really blame him for that.'

'I hadn't finished,' Holly said haughtily. 'He's also wearing dark glasses. I mean, really huge black sunglasses. In this weather! Talk about dramatic. What's he got to hide anyway?'

Anna tutted. 'Maybe, as Rachel said, he's got a headache. Honestly, Holly, you're such a drama queen.'

'Suit yourself. You wouldn't say that if you saw him,' Holly assured her. 'There's something not right about him. He's all edgy-looking. Do you think he's on drugs? I think he's on drugs.'

'Well, luckily, nobody asked you for a diagnosis, so go back to the reception desk and be polite.'

Holly tutted, and headed back into Reception. Rachel turned back to Anna, an apologetic expression on her face. 'So, as I was saying, I'm ever so sorry about being late, but the weirdest thing happened this morning, and — ' She broke off as Holly returned.

'He wants to know how long you're going to be. Says he can't wait forever. I told him you're about to call your first patient and he's second on the list, but he says it's an emergency.'

'An emergency?' Rachel raised an eyebrow. 'Thought it was a new patient check?'

'It is. But the funny thing is — oh, hang on.' Holly rushed back into Reception as an elderly female voice called, 'Excuse me, dear. Anyone there?'

Anna patted Rachel's arm. 'I can see you're in a bit of a flap, and I'm sure you have a good explanation for why you were late, but it can wait. Let's get the queue down first, shall we?'

Rachel nodded glumly, and turned to the door, only to hear Holly's voice calling to her. She halted in her tracks, and Holly rushed up to her, saying quietly, 'That was Mrs Wicks. She's your first appointment. She said you can call the mystery man in first. Get it over and done with.'

'Really? Why's that?'

'She's a bit worried about him,' Holly said, grinning. 'Thinks he's *one of them heroin addicts who needs his fix*. Told you he looked all edgy, didn't I? You must find out all about him and tell us when you get a moment. You know, there's something vaguely familiar about him. When he came to the desk just now, I went all goosepimply. His voice especially. I don't recognise the name, but even so . . . '

Rachel laughed. 'He's here for a new patient check-up, not an interrogation.' As Holly pulled a disappointed face, she headed back to her consulting room. If she did find out anything, she thought mischievously, she might well keep it to herself, just to annoy Holly. Not that she expected to make any exciting discoveries, anyway. He was just a bloke with a headache, probably. Anyway, she had more important things to worry about.

Her smile disappeared when she thought about the text she'd had from her mum.

HORSE IN PADDOCK. LOOKS MUCH HAPPIER. CAN'T FIND GROOMING EQUIP-MENT THOUGH. SEE YOU LATER. X

Rachel tutted. Her mother knew barely anything about horses. It was her dad who'd run the farm. Her mum was a townie through and through, and had spent her working life in a bookshop in Helmston. Why she was suddenly acting as if animals were the be-all and end-all, Rachel couldn't imagine. Then her face crumpled. Of course she knew why. Animals on the farm reminded her mum of happier times, before it all went so badly wrong. When Folly Farm was still a working dairy farm. When Rachel's dad was still around, the picture of health and vitality. When Rachel's mum had complained about the mud, told her father nearly every day that she must have been mad to fall in love with a farmer. When they'd all laughed a lot, and loved each other fiercely, in spite of the hardships and worries.

She pushed open the door of her consulting room, telling herself it was silly to worry about her mum being at home while she was at work. After all, she'd been living alone for three years, and now she had Rachel and Sam sharing her home. Surely that had to be better for her? And, anyway, Rachel always nipped home at lunchtime to check on her, and often rang her during morning and afternoon breaks. Just . . . she'd aged so much lately, and she seemed so low, so — so lost.

She really hoped she hadn't put herself in any danger with that horse. It had seemed friendly enough, but you just never knew. The kindest, sweetest creature could become violent, sometimes without any warning, any provocation. Just for the sheer hell of it . . .

She shivered, and forced herself to concentrate on the task in hand. Settling herself at the desk, she re-entered her password to unlock the computer screen. She quickly found the mystery patient on the system and scanned through the notes from his previous surgery. Not much to show. No long-term conditions, or family history of any significance. He wasn't on any health registers; no asthma, diabetes, or heart disease. He wasn't even on any repeat medication. His check-up should be pretty straightforward. She glanced at his address. Sweet Briar Cottage. Wasn't that the pretty thatched cottage on the outskirts of Bramblewick? The one with the whitewashed walls and latticed windows — like something off the cover of a chocolate box. It stood out in her memory, because you didn't get many thatched cottages in that area. Fancy him living there.

She shrugged to herself. What did it matter? She had a job to do, so enough with the speculation. Time to call him through.

*   *   *

Xander jumped when the name flashed across the screen of the electronic notice board above the rack of NHS leaflets in the waiting room. *Alexander South*. He'd almost forgotten he was called that, and had nearly given the wrong name when he'd registered at the surgery a couple of weeks ago.

He took note of the room number

and strode purposefully down the corridor. The sooner this was over and done with, the better.

He tapped on the door, heard a muffled 'Come in,' and pushed it open. A woman, probably around his own age, wearing a rather unflattering navy-blue tunic and matching trousers, glanced up from the computer and gave him a brief smile. 'Come in. Take a seat.'

She waved a hand in the direction of the chair at the side of her desk, and he sat, feeling suddenly nervous. He'd only been registered at his previous surgery for a few months, and it seemed desperately unfair that he had to have yet another health check. He was sick of them, to be frank. In America, they were obsessed with them. At times, he'd felt like a human pin cushion. Surveying the stethoscope, sample bottles and other nursing paraphernalia, he felt a rising irritability. Why was everything always so complicated? The world was wrapped up tightly in red tape.

She finally looked away from the screen and smiled again. 'So, Mr South. How are you today?'

'Mm, fine,' he mumbled.

She raised an eyebrow. 'No headache or anything like that?'

He frowned. Why should he have a headache?

As if she'd read his thoughts, she made circular motions in front of her eyes, and he remembered that he was wearing his sunglasses. No wonder this room looked so gloomy. 'Oh, oh yeah. Right.'

Reluctantly, he pulled them from his face and tucked them into his top pocket, then looked up at her, almost defiantly. Expecting her eyes to widen in recognition, he was somewhat unnerved when she seemed to rear away from him. For a split second he could have sworn he saw fear in her eyes, but then it was gone, and she said, perfectly calmly, 'That's better. I can see who I'm talking to now.'

His eyebrows knitted together. He

must have been imagining it. So, she didn't recognise him? Well, that was good. Unusual, but good. Refreshing, even. He began to relax.

'Have you brought your sample of urine?' She'd pulled on some gloves, and held out a hand, and he fumbled in his pocket, flushing slightly as he removed the bottle he'd been given when he registered. How embarrassing.

She unscrewed the cap and dipped something in the bottle. He looked away, feeling awkward, and also a little worried. What if she found something wrong?

'Excellent,' she said. He glanced up as she headed over to the sink and removed her gloves. He gulped and began to study a poster on the wall, all about childhood immunisations. He heard the flip of a bin lid, then the sound of a tap running, followed by several paper towels being torn from the dispenser. The bin flipped again, then she was taking her seat beside him.

He risked looking back at her, and

saw that she was tapping something else into the computer. She glanced round, catching him looking at her. She smiled again, and he realised she had dimples, and dark eyes which were watching him with a most peculiar expression — one he simply couldn't fathom.

'Don't look so worried,' she said. 'It's all very simple. Can you take your coat off for me, and roll up your shirt sleeve?'

He nodded, annoyed with himself. She'd think he was a total wimp at this rate, and he wasn't. Was he? Mind you, he thought ruefully, trying to stay calm as she wrapped a cuff around his arm and took his blood pressure, it made a refreshing change for a woman to think he was a wimp. Usually they expected far too much from him. It inevitably led to disappointment. Whoever Bay Curtis was, Alexander South was a very different man.

'Nothing wrong with that, anyway. Can I just weigh you and check your height, please?' she said, standing up.

26

He obliged, slightly disgruntled to find that he'd gained four pounds since he was last weighed. He'd have to watch that. He stood under the measuring guide. 'I'm six-three,' he informed her, his voice croaky. Probably because he hadn't spoken for a couple of days. Well, apart from murmured conversations with his dogs.

'Hmm. Six-two,' she said, heading back to the desk.

He pulled a face. *That's not what it says on Wikipedia.* 'I think your equipment's faulty,' he informed her.

She raised an eyebrow, and he felt suddenly incredibly foolish. What a stupid thing to say! As if it mattered.

He sat down again, and she began to ask him questions about his health history.

'Do you smoke?'

Not since I was fourteen, and my father caught me taking a sneaky drag behind the garden shed, and forced me to chain-smoke a pack of twenty. He could still taste them when he thought about it. Never touched them since. 'Definitely not. Filthy habit.'

'Do you drink alcohol?'

Was she kidding? Didn't everyone drink alcohol? Even if it was just a sherry at Christmas like his nan. What did she mean? She should be more specific. 'Occasionally.'

'What do you mean by 'occasionally'?'

All right, Kommandant, don't shine a light in my eyes. 'You know — a glass of wine with dinner, maybe a nightcap now and then, the odd pint in a pub at the weekend. Not every weekend,' he added hastily. Not by a long chalk, he reflected gloomily. He'd hardly been out at all for simply *ages*.

He answered her questions as honestly as he could, wondering if they were ever going to end. Finally, she turned away from the computer and said, 'Okay, just going to take a little sample of blood from you.'

Xander swallowed. He'd heard that before. Usually it meant they were going to take buckets of the stuff. He hated having his blood taken. Just the thought of it made him go all funny, and his knees felt quite weak. 'Is that really necessary?'

She frowned. 'It won't take a moment. Do you have a needle phobia?'

He tried to look cool. 'Certainly not.'

'Great. Not a problem, then.' She was writing on a white card with a polythene pocket attached. He knew the sample bottles would go inside that pocket. There'd be bottles and bottles of his blood sitting in there. He felt queasy, and bit his lip.

'Are you a good bleeder?' She was pulling on a fresh pair of gloves.

Xander looked away, studying the *Stop Smoking* poster on the far wall with remarkable interest, considering he was a non-smoker. 'I presume so.' He shrugged. 'I've never had any complaints.'

She put a pillow under his arm and told him to make a fist.

As she attached a tourniquet to his

arm, he flexed his hand as she'd showed him, and studied her face. It was a kind face, he decided, but she was tired. He could see it in her eyes. And there was tension in her mouth. He wondered what her story was.

'Okay, just a scratch.'

He looked hastily away again, feeling his legs turn to jelly as the needle entered his arm and she began to draw the blood from him. He distracted himself by creating a backstory for her. He'd just decided that she was thirty-five, had three kids, lived with an unappreciative partner who wouldn't marry her (no wedding ring), and was sick of being stuck in this remote moorland village and longed for the bright lights of the city . . . when she smiled suddenly and said, 'All done. Just hold this cotton wool over it a moment.'

He did as she asked, not looking over to the desk in case he saw all the tubes filled with the blood that she'd just drained from him. She stuck a piece of tape over the cotton wool ball.

'That wasn't too bad, was it?' She gave him a knowing look. 'Does it hurt? The eye, I mean.'

His hand automatically flew to his face, and he touched his cheekbone, rather tentatively. 'Not at all,' he lied. He'd completely forgotten about the black eye. He'd been so worried about being recognised that he hadn't given it a second thought. No wonder she'd looked at him so oddly when he took off his sunglasses.

She arched an eyebrow, and he grinned sheepishly. 'Well, maybe a bit. But not as much as it did.'

Her lips definitely tightened, and he felt a sudden need to explain. 'I don't make a habit of it, you know. Fighting. I'm really not that sort of man.'

'I wasn't judging,' she assured him, suddenly all official and brisk. 'It's none of my business.'

He felt deflated and couldn't say why. 'I know. Just that — '

Just that *what?* What did it matter

what some practice nurse thought of him, anyway? Besides, he had more important things to worry about. He glanced at the clock on the wall and pulled a face. 'Thank you. Am I dismissed?'

She nodded. 'Call back in a few days for your blood test results. If there's anything major we'll be in touch, but don't worry. I'm sure you're perfect.'

It was his turn to look amused as her face flooded with colour. 'I mean, your *results*. I'm sure you're in perfect *health.*'

He stood up, rolled his shirt sleeve down, and pulled on his coat. 'Thank you, Nurse.' He peered at her name badge and smiled. 'Nurse Rachel. It was a pleasure to meet you.' He held out his hand, and she shook it lightly, her eyes fixed on his. She had very long, black lashes, soft, creamy skin, and wavy brown hair, fastened securely in a ponytail. 'So, I'll call back at the end of the week?'

'Yes, yes, that should be okay.'

He let go of her hand, nodded kindly at her and left the room. As he entered the waiting room, a little old lady passed him. She gave him a very suspicious look and made a determined effort to give him a wide berth. He realised he'd forgotten to put his sunglasses back on. Poor old dear was probably thinking he was about to mug her. Great impression he was making in the village already. And now he had to go and sort out the little matter of Fred, and throw himself on the mercy of complete strangers. So much for the peace and quiet of the country.

3

There was a Land Rover in the yard as Rachel pulled into Folly Farm that lunchtime. As if on cue, the farmhouse door opened, and her mother stepped out behind an elderly chap in wellies and a waxed jacket.

'Rachel, I didn't realise the time!' Her mum clapped her hands together. 'I'm so sorry. I haven't made you any dinner yet.'

Rachel shook her head. She wasn't hungry. A nice cup of tea would do just fine. She glanced at the man, who gave her a warm smile. 'It doesn't matter, Mum. I can see you've been busy.'

'Ah, yes. It's been quite a morning.' Her mother, Rachel noticed with some surprise, looked quite animated. Almost like her old self. 'Rachel, you remember Merlyn, our vet? He's been to see Fred.'

'Fred? Who the — ' Rachel sighed.

'You mean the horse? You've given him a name?'

'Not me. I met the owner. He came over this morning to introduce himself and apologise. It's quite a story.'

'I'll bet it is,' Rachel muttered. 'Hello, Merlyn. You're still working, then? Can't believe that!'

'Not ready to be put out to pasture just yet, although my young partner is itching to take over the reins, so to speak. He'll just have to wait a while.'

'Good for you.' Merlyn was a wonderful vet, she remembered. Her dad had thought highly of him. 'So, is the horse ill?'

Merlyn shook his head. 'Not ill, no. A little underweight, certainly. He's been tethered on council land over the winter, I understand. I see it far too often lately. They can't move away to fresh grass when they need it, and many don't get enough hay either. There's plenty of good spring grass in your paddock, but I'd be wary of him eating too much. My feeling is, until he adjusts, let him graze freely for a couple of hours in the morning, then either bring him indoors or put him in a grazing muzzle after that. We don't know anything about him or his medical history, and we don't want the poor chap to get laminitis. Bring him in at night, give him a net of hay, and we'll keep monitoring him, see how he goes. He's not dangerously underweight, and I don't think it will take long for him to recover condition. Many horses slim off over the winter. I've checked his teeth and there are no problems there, so that's not stopping him eating. His feet need some attention and his hooves need trimming, but we're on the case, and I've wormed him. With a bit of loving care, he should be right as rain soon enough.'

'The farrier's coming this afternoon,' her mother added brightly. 'He's going to trim his hooves. He's offered to help me groom him, too. He'll be as good as new by tonight.'

The vet grinned. 'Well, maybe it will

take a bit longer than that, but he's clearly in safe hands; and, as I said, we'll keep monitoring him. He should be fine.'

'Thanks to his heroic rescuer.'

'Quite. I'll bid you good day, Janie. Any problems, just give me a call.' He nodded over at Rachel. 'Nice to see you again, Rachel.'

As he jumped into his Land Rover, Rachel turned to her mother, her eyes wide with incredulity. 'You're keeping the horse?'

'Fred. His name's Fred. His rescuer named him.'

'His rescuer clearly has a distinct lack of imagination. What on earth's going on?'

'Why don't you come inside, love? It's freezing out here. I'll warm you up some tomato soup and put the kettle on, then I'll explain everything.'

The farmhouse kitchen felt positively toasty after the cold March air outside. Rachel sank into the tatty old chair by the range and tried to resist the urge to make the soup and tea herself. Her mum would only get resentful and remind her that she wasn't dead yet. It was, after all, her kitchen. Besides, Rachel worked hard at the surgery, and Mrs Frost liked to think of the farmhouse as her domain. It was just so difficult, after Rachel had become used to doing everything for herself and Sam.

She leaned back and closed her eyes wearily. 'So, are you going to fill me in?'

She opened her eyes again as Mrs Frost scraped a kitchen chair along the slate floor and sat down beside her. 'It's such a heartbreaking story, Rachel. Heartbreaking, but incredibly uplifting, too. You see, there was this young man who — ' She broke off at a knock on the door.

'Don't tell me,' Rachel said, heaving herself out of the chair. 'This is the farrier. How much is all this costing, Mum? And who's paying for it all, that's what I want to know.'

She could see the shape of someone tall through the frosted glass pane in the farmhouse door. She pulled the door open and stared into a pair of dark sunglasses. 'You!'

She couldn't see his eyes but could tell he was shocked by the way his mouth fell open. 'You!'

Her mother appeared behind her and peered over Rachel's shoulder. 'Mr South, how lovely to see you again. This is my daughter, Rachel. Please, please come in.' She turned and hurried back inside.

He smiled faintly. 'It's Xander, remember?' he called, then shrugged. 'Hello again, Rachel.'

Rachel stepped aside reluctantly and allowed her mother's visitor inside, feeling confused. Her patient was the farrier?

'I was making a cup of tea,' her mum said as they entered the kitchen. 'You're just in time. Bet you heard me put the kettle on, didn't you?' She gave him an affectionate smile and Rachel blinked. Whoever he was, he'd certainly won her mother over. She wondered if he'd revealed his black eye to her yet. That might change her mum's opinion of him.

As if she'd read her daughter's thoughts, Mrs Frost paused in making the tea and said, 'I was just thinking, Mr South, you ought to let Rachel take a look at that eye. She's a nurse, you know.'

He removed his glasses and he and Rachel looked at each other warily. 'I'm sure it's nothing worth worrying about,' he said. 'It'll be fine in a few days. It's not my first black eye.'

'Like a good fight, do you?' she snapped at him, then cursed herself. She shouldn't judge. But then again, she reasoned, she wasn't in surgery now. She was entitled to an opinion. And male aggression made her sick. Literally. She really didn't want the soup any more. Her stomach was churning.

He shook his head slightly. 'Not particularly. Sometimes, we don't have a choice.'

'There's always a choice,' she said coldly.

He hesitated. 'You're right, I suppose,' he said eventually. 'Let's just say, sometimes it's the right choice.'

'That's a cop-out,' she told him bluntly.

'Rachel!' Her mother slammed a cup of tea on the table in front of her and glared at her. 'Don't be so rude.'

'It's fine, Mrs Frost.' Mr South held up his hand. 'Perhaps I should leave.'

'Certainly not. Here, drink your tea,' she replied, handing him a mug with a great deal more gentleness than when she'd given Rachel hers. 'Rachel, sit down. Your soup's nearly ready. Would you like some soup, Mr South?'

He shook his head. 'Thank you, but no. I only came to see if the vet had been yet. And please, call me Xander.'

'Well, Xander, you'd be very welcome to have something to eat. It is dinner time, you know, and I'd be only too happy to open another tin.'

Rachel's lips pursed mutinously. Why was her mother fawning over this no-hoper? She stared at him, taking in every detail of him as he smiled up at her mum, assuring her that he wasn't hungry and really hadn't meant to interrupt their lunch, and couldn't apologise enough for all the inconvenience he'd caused. He was very well-spoken. Quite posh, in fact. He had short, straight, fair hair which he'd brushed back from his face, and a neat, trimmed, fair beard. Behind the bruises his eyes were blue, and rather serious.

'So, I take it you're the owner of our unexpected guest?' She heard the coldness in her tone and picked up her mug of tea, feeling embarrassed. Her mother was eyeing her in the way she used to when Rachel was a wilful teenager, about to launch into Stern Mum mode.

Xander turned to her. 'I am, I suppose. At least, unofficially. But I really can't see his previous owner coming to claim him, even if he can find him.'

'I should hope not,' Mrs Frost exclaimed, quite distracted from telling off her daughter. 'Mind you, if he did I'd be calling the police. Make no mistake about that.'

'Would someone like to tell me what's been going on?' Rachel rubbed her forehead, feeling exhausted. She had to be back at work in a short while, and she hadn't even started eating her soup — which, she realised suddenly, she appeared to have regained an appetite for.

Her mum sat down at the table opposite her. 'Mr South — I mean, Xander — rescued Fred last night. You'll never believe it, Rachel, how cruel some men can be.'

Rachel spooned sugar into her tea. She could quite well believe it. It was her mother who would be astounded, which was why she'd never hear it from Rachel. 'What happened?'

'I'd been out with friends last night. They live in Kearton Bay, so it was good to have a catch-up, and, well, we ended up in a nightclub in Oddborough. Charlie wasn't feeling well, so they left quite early, and I decided to get something to eat, then get a taxi home.' He paused, obviously noting the look of disapproval on her face. 'I wasn't drunk, if that's what you're thinking.'

'Nothing to do with me if you were,' she said coldly, holding up her hands. 'Your life, your business.'

He stared at her a moment. 'Yes, I suppose it is,' he said. 'Anyway, they'd recommended a fabulous Indian restaurant just outside Whitby, so I got a cab there. Afterwards, I thought I'd walk into Whitby to get a taxi home, and on the way there, I heard a bit of a commotion coming from the railway line. You know, the main Oddborough-to-Whitby track?'

Rachel said nothing. He sighed, then glanced at Mrs Frost, who seemed to decide she would finish the story for him.

'Some rogue — and I'm being very polite there — was only trying to pull poor Fred onto the track.' She shook her head. 'Have you ever heard anything more inhumane?'

Rachel's mouth dropped open. 'What? Are you sure?'

'Of course I'm sure,' Xander said. 'You should have heard the language he was using, hauling poor old Fred forward. I think Fred knew what was in store for him, because he'd dug his hooves in well and truly, and was refusing to budge. There was a toolbag on the track. The man had actually broken a hole in the fence to get the horse through.'

'But — but why? Who would do something so vile?'

'I asked him that. Eventually. We had a bit of a tussle first.' He gave a rueful grin and gestured to his eye. 'This was the result.'

Rachel shifted uncomfortably. Maybe she'd misjudged Xander, after all. She couldn't say she blamed him for fighting with someone like that. 'And?'

'He reckoned he couldn't afford to keep the horse, and it was the kindest way. Said Fred had been grazing on council land in Oddborough. According to him, there are horses all over the place, tethered on roadside verges and any bit of grassland lying empty. But the council's planning to build on that land, and he was being threatened with fines and prosecution, so he thought he'd avoid all that by helping Fred to meet his maker.'

'Couldn't he have found him another home? Rung a sanctuary, or something?'

'He reckoned he's tried two horse sanctuaries, and both said they were full to bursting and couldn't take any more. They recommended he ring the RSPCA.'

'Then why didn't he?'

'He didn't say, but I reckon it's because he was worried they would prosecute him, because Fred has clearly been neglected. He's filthy and underweight, and his feet definitely haven't been looked after. I think he was scared he'd end up in court, so decided to take matters into his own hands instead.'

'Oh, good grief! That's appalling.' Rachel blinked away tears, trying not to imagine the terrible fate that could have awaited Fred, had Xander not chanced upon him — not to mention the danger to the people on any train that might have hit him. Always supposing he hadn't been electrocuted first. 'But how on earth did you end up bringing him here?'

Xander took a sip of tea and leaned back in his chair. 'It was a flash of memory. Years ago, when I was just a kid, I stayed just outside Bramblewick with my grandparents. They'd rented a holiday cottage, and Grandad used to take me to a farm every morning for fresh eggs for breakfast.' He gave her a smile that revealed he had dimples. 'Folly Farm. I remembered it when I was standing there last night, holding a halter rope and wondering what on earth I was going to do with this horse. The bloke had run off and it had started to rain, and I just thought, *Okay, best get walking.*'

Rachel gasped. 'Walking! You walked all the way from outside Whitby? In the rain?' And it really had rained yesterday evening, she remembered. It had poured down, hammering on her windows all night. No wonder she hadn't heard the sound of hooves.

'I really didn't know what else to do. Then, of course, when I got here, it was the early hours of the morning and the house was in darkness. I couldn't see any sign of other animals. To be honest, I wouldn't even have known anyone still lived here if it hadn't been for your car parked in the yard. But the loose box was just there, and I thought if I could just get him inside and safe for the night, I could deal with everything in the morning. Luckily, there was a bucket in the stables and an outside tap, so I could give him water. I was worried sick about him, just leaving him there with no food, but I couldn't see a thing, and I didn't want to turn him out into a field without checking it was secure, or that there was nothing lying around or growing that could hurt him. I couldn't wait to get back to him this morning, but I had to be somewhere else first thing.' He lifted his eyebrows at her, and she nodded.

'I see.'

'I'm terribly sorry you got involved in all this,' he said. 'Obviously, I'll be paying the vet bill and farrier bill, and I will pay for livery costs.'

'So, we're keeping him here?'

He glanced at Mrs Frost, his voice suddenly uncertain. 'Well, your mother said — '

'Of course we're keeping him here,' her mum cut in. 'It will be lovely to have a horse on the farm, and Sam will love it. He was hoping he'd stay.'

'Sam?'

'My son,' Rachel said curtly. She didn't want to get into conversations with Xander South about her family life. 'Is that soup nearly ready, Mum? Only I have to be back at work soon.'

'Of course, love. Coming right up.' Mrs Frost reached for a bowl from the cupboard. 'Are you sure you won't have some, Xander?'

'No, honestly. Thank you.' He stood

up, scraping back his chair. 'I'll just pop out and say hello to Fred, then I really must be going. I do appreciate your help in this, Mrs Frost. Yours too, Rachel. I'll pop by this afternoon, after the farrier's been, and settle with you for any costs. You did give the vet my address?'

'I did, love. You'll be getting the bill, don't you worry.' Mrs Frost laughed. 'Nothing too drastic, though. It was just a check-up and the worming. You won't have to sell your body to pay the bills.'

He grinned at her, and glanced over at Rachel; who, unaccountably, found her face was burning. 'I'll say good day, then. No doubt we'll be seeing each other again soon.'

'Oh, I'm usually at work,' she said quickly. 'I'm sure my mum will be happy to help with whatever you — or, rather, Fred — needs.'

He hesitated, as if about to say something, but seemed to think better of it. 'Please, no need to show me out. I know the way. Good day, Mrs Frost. Rachel.'

Then he was gone, and the kitchen felt suddenly very big and very empty. Mrs Frost put the bowl of soup down in front of her and folded her arms. 'Well, that was a bit weird, wasn't it?'

'I think it was,' Rachel agreed, picking up her spoon. 'What was he doing, walking to Whitby at that time of night, anyway?'

Her mother tutted. 'I was talking about you. What an attitude! Time you remembered your manners, young lady.'

4

The Bay Horse was warm and cosy and, as she sat back in her chair, glass of white wine in hand, Rachel began to relax for the first time in what felt like forever. She'd almost said no to Anna's invitation. A drink after work on the Friday night seemed like too much effort. Besides, Anna had invited her friends along, and Rachel didn't know them — well, apart from Holly, of course. Then there was Sam and her mum to think of, and she was so tired.

It had been her mother who'd talked her into going. 'About time you got out and enjoyed yourself. You've been through a hard time, what with the separation and everything, and all the stress of moving up here. Get yourself that pub and have some fun for a ge. Sam will be fine with me.'

hel closed her eyes, took a sip of

wine, and reflected that her mother was quite right. She had been through a hard time — harder than her mum could ever imagine. But so had Sam. And it was Sam she worried about more than anyone.

As if Anna had read her thoughts, she tapped Rachel on the arm. 'So, how's Sam settling in? Does he like his new school?'

Rachel sat up straight, automatically on guard. 'He seems to be okay.' She smiled nervously at Anna's friend Izzy, who was sitting opposite her. 'I suppose you'll know better than I do if he's settling in at school?'

She'd been rather disconcerted, upon arriving at The Bay Horse, to discover that one of Anna's best friends was none other than Sam's new teacher. Izzy, though, seemed friendly enough, and was keen to reassure Rachel that Sam was just fine. 'He's a bright boy, no doubt about that.' She hesitate 'He's a bit quiet, but I think that's c to be expected. It's always diff adjusting to a new school, making new friends. I'm sure he'll find his feet very quickly.'

Rachel felt a lurch of anxiety. 'What do you mean, quiet?'

Izzy looked surprised. 'You know, a bit shy, maybe. It's hard for children who arrive at a new school where everyone else has known each other for years — especially in a small school like Bramblewick.'

'But does he seem to fit in? Is he mixing at all? Do the other children seem okay with him?'

Anna and Izzy exchanged glances. 'He's not being bullied, if that's what you're worried about. Honestly, Rachel, relax. It's just a question of settling in, that's all.'

Anna gave her a sympathetic smile. 'I do know how you feel. I worry all the time about my stepdaughter, and I now Connor was a mass of nerves hen she started at the school. She was te arrival too, you see. And it was worse for her, and for Connor.'

'Oh? Why would it be worse for her than it is for Sam?' Rachel heard the sharpness in her tone and her face heated up. She had to stop being so sensitive. Maybe, one day, the guilt would ease, and she would be able to act like a normal mother. She couldn't even imagine it.

'Gracie — my stepdaughter — is on the autism spectrum. She had quite a time adjusting to a new start in Bramblewick — ' Anna glanced at her friends, who all nodded in agreement. ' — but she got there in the end. It's not plain sailing by any means, but her teacher is amazing with her, and we take it one day at a time.'

Rachel felt ashamed. 'I'm sorry. I didn't mean to be rude. I get a bit defensive about Sam . . . ' Her voice trailed off and she took a large gulp of wine.

Nell, a curvy blonde with big blue eyes and a warm smile, patted her arm kindly. 'You weren't being rude,' assured her. 'I should think it's na to worry about your child starting a new school.'

'And you're getting a divorce, aren't you?' Holly said, picking up her glass of vodka. 'I expect there's loads of guilt attached to that. Divorce is a minefield, isn't it? And Sam probably misses his dad, so you'll be worrying about that, too.'

Rachel swallowed, aware that the others were giving Holly meaningful looks. Rachel had only worked with Holly for three weeks, but she'd already realised that her colleague wasn't the most tactful of people. She tended to say whatever popped into her mind, and only think about it afterwards when it was too late.

'I hope you never decide to become a counsellor, Holls,' Izzy said cheerfully. 'Take no notice of her, Rachel. She opens her mouth before she engages her brain. Now, shall we change the subject? No offence to you and Anna, but I'm surrounded by kids all week, and when I work I like to forget about them.'

'Sounds good to me,' Ne~~~ agreed.

Holly shrugged. 'Sorry. I d~~~'t mean to offend.'

'You didn't,' Rachel said, holdi~~ the stem of her glass tightly, 'but I th~~k Izzy's right. Let's talk about something else.'

Anna glanced over at the bar. 'Where's Matt tonight, anyway?' she asked. 'Matt's Izzy's boyfriend,' she explained to Rachel. 'His mum and dad run the pub and he lives here.'

'Don't call him my boyfriend. Sounds like we're soppy teenagers. He's gone bowling in Helmston with his new work-mates.' Izzy rolled her eyes. 'You know what it's like when you have a new job — socialising with people you've nothing in common with, just to fit in.' Her gaze fell on Rachel and her face turned scarlet with embarrassment. 'I didn't mean you, obviously, Rachel. That wasn't meant — oh, heck!'

Rachel couldn't help laughing, seeing the look on Izzy's face. 'It's okay. I kno~ exactly what you mean. I had serio~

doubts out coming out tonight myself, but I' quite glad I did. It's a nice pub, and 'e company isn't bad — if you ign' e everyone's habit of putting their f ot in it every time they open their mouths!'

Nell laughed too. 'Sometimes I'm very glad I'm my own boss,' she said. 'I dodge all these office politics.'

'What do you do, Nell?' Rachel enquired.

'Have you seen Spill the Beans, just down the road?'

Rachel nodded. 'The coffee shop and bakery? Yes. I popped in there yesterday for a cake for Sam and Mum. It used to be Carlton's Bakery when I lived here years ago. Certainly gone upmarket since then. So, is that your place?'

Nell nodded proudly. 'Yep. And I bake everything we sell — well, almost everything. I have a fabulous assistant, Chloe. She must have served you yesterday. She's almost as good as I am t baking. Almost. Not so good at the ke decorating, though, unfortunately.'

'But you have the hunk...
you out there,' Izzy giggled...
at icing a cupcake, is Riley,...
startled Rachel. 'Would you be...

'Riley?' Rachel wondered if sh...
having her on. 'You mean *our* Riley?'
She glanced at Anna. 'Dr MacDonald?'

'*My* Riley, actually,' Nell said, a big grin on her face. 'And yes, he's pretty good at it. You look surprised.'

'I am,' Rachel admitted. Riley was a big, burly, redheaded Scotsman, and seemed as likely to be an accomplished cake decorator as Rachel was to win the Badminton Horse Trials. 'He, er, doesn't seem the type.'

'He's full of surprises,' Nell said, sounding dreamy.

Anna laughed. 'Ignore her, Rachel. She's absolutely smitten with him.'

'You can talk,' Holly said, pushing away an empty packet of crisps and longingly eyeing Anna's unopened pack that lay on the table. 'Anna and Connor only got married at Christmas, s...
they're still in the flush of new love, ar...

...n the besotted stage with ...estly, Rachel, it's a relief you're ...ere. I always feel like the sad singl...n when I'm out with this lot.'

Izzy's Matt.

Rachel shifted uncomfortably. She didn't want the conversation to go down the path of relationships. There would be too many questions. 'As I said, I wasn't going to come out tonight at all. You have my mum to thank for not being the only single girl here. She insisted I came out, and you can never argue with your mum, can you?' She kept her tone deliberately light, hoping to change the direction of the conversation.

'How is your mum, anyway?' Anna asked, to her relief. 'She hasn't been to the surgery for ages — which is a good thing, obviously. I hardly ever see her these days. My dad was very fond of her.'

Rachel remembered her mother telling her, during one of her flying visits just after her father died, that Dr Gray had been a godsend, and kindness itself, visiting her every day to check up on her and even bringing the shopping to her at the farm. She felt a familiar pang of guilt. She should have been there for her mum more, after her father's death. If only she'd been able to break free sooner. If only she'd had the courage. If only . . . 'Mum was very fond of him, too. He was so good to her after Dad died. She'd have been lost without him.'

'I liked your dad,' Anna said, her eyes kind. 'He was a good man. It was such a shame, what happened. Losing his livelihood like that.'

'He was never the same after the herd went,' Rachel murmured. 'Dratted foot-and-mouth.'

It had wiped out many farmers, she recalled. 2001 — the year when everything changed for her family. It had been the final straw for her already struggling father. She remembered the horror of that year: The burning pyres of dead cattle and sheep, the closed footpaths, the foot baths in the car park in the village, the warnings and Keep Out notices posted at strategic points. The North York Moors had suffered badly, once a case was confirmed on a farm not far from Bramblewick, but it certainly wasn't alone. The whole country had been hit. Farmers all across the land devastated, herds isolated, restricted, destroyed, the rural economy plunged into crisis as tourists stayed away and small businesses dependent on visitors struggled to survive. Some farmers rebuilt afterwards, using the compensation they'd received to restock and start again. Some, however, decided they'd had enough. They'd been finding it difficult to keep going, even before the foot-and-mouth crisis, and the outbreak was the last straw. Her father, devastated at the loss of his herd, had been one of them.

Rachel had heard him one night, talking to her mother in a low voice in the kitchen. 'It might have been different if I thought Rachel wanted to take over one day, but we both know that will never happen. She's set on becoming a nurse, and who can blame her? This is no life for any lass — or any lad, come to that. When I'm gone, there'll be no one to run the place, any road, so best let it go now.'

'But what will you do?' Her mother had sounded tearful, and Rachel had bitten her lip to stop herself from crying, feeling torn with guilt that she wasn't the son or daughter her father had needed — the sort who dreamed of nothing more than taking over the family farm.

'Put me feet up,' her dad had replied, trying to sound jovial. 'Let you keep me, for a change. We'll manage, love. You've still got your job, and maybe I can get work on a farm round here. There's allus someone needs summat doing.'

'And the farm?'

'It's our home. I'll not sell up, if that's what you're worrying about. I'll maybe rent some of the land out, but Folly Farm stays in our family, no matter what.'

It had been some comfort, at the

time, to know that her home wasn't going to be sold from under her feet; but Rachel sometimes wondered, as time passed, if it would have been easier if it had been. With the farm buildings empty, and the yard silent, her dad had changed. She'd noticed a difference every time she'd gone home during her breaks from university. She'd worried about him while she was away, wondering how he was coping, what he was doing with his time. Maybe that was what had made her vulnerable to Grant's charms. He'd seemed so caring back then, so concerned. He'd listened to her worries and understood them. She'd been hooked before she'd even realised it.

'What's your mum doing with herself these days?'

Rachel blinked as Izzy's voice penetrated her thoughts. 'Oh, you know, pottering about. Sam is her new project. She adores him, and I think it's been great for her to have him around.'

Her mum had been alone too long, she reflected. Rattling around in that big farmhouse, with only memories to sustain her. She tried hard to push the guilt aside. She was back home now. She would make her mum happy again, whatever it took. And she certainly seemed brighter with Rachel and Sam to care for, and now Fred . . .

'She's got a horse,' she blurted out, more for something to say than any real desire to impart the information. 'Fred. At least, he's not really her horse, but we're keeping him at Folly Farm for someone, and it's really cheered Mum up.'

'Ooh, in'esting.' Holly shuffled on her seat, her mouth full of stolen salt-and-vinegar crisps. 'Who hore i'it?'

Anna pulled a face. 'At least swallow your crisps — *my* crisps — before you speak, Holls. That looks disgusting.' She turned to Rachel. 'I think what she was trying to say was, whose horse is it?'

Rachel flushed. Maybe this wasn't such a great topic of conversation after all. She'd momentarily forgotten Holly's interest in the 'mystery patient'.

This was going to start all manner of speculation.

Sure enough, Holly was agog. 'So that's why he was wearing sunglasses! Fancy fighting over a horse. What a hero.'

'It's unbelievable.' Nell's eyes brimmed with tears. 'Who'd do something like that to a poor defenceless animal?'

'Lots of people, unfortunately,' Anna said with a sigh. 'There are abandoned horses all over the place, and the sanctuaries can't cope. People can buy a horse cheaply, but then they realise they can't afford the feed, the vet bills, the insurance . . . They just dump them. And there are lots of people who can't — or won't — meet livery or grazing costs, so they turn them out onto any spare patch of land. I've even seen horses grazing on roadside verges. Terrifies the life out of me. It's such a shame.'

'I always wanted a horse when I was a kid,' Holly admitted. 'Of course, it was never going to happen. We could never have afforded it.' She smiled at Rachel. 'I'm glad our crazy patient turned out to be a good guy, and I'm really glad your mum took Fred in.'

In spite of her misgivings, Rachel smiled back. 'So am I. It's given Mum a new lease of life. I haven't seen her so enthusiastic for ages. She misses having animals on the farm. Funny, really, because she was never involved with the animals when Dad was running the place. She was quite happy with her job at the bookshop in Helmston and taking care of the house. I suppose she just got accustomed to hearing the noise of the farmyard. It must seem very quiet now.'

'What's he like, anyway?' Holly's voice was curious, which was just what Rachel had feared when she'd broached the subject of Fred.

'Big, hairy, skinny. He's been wormed, though, and his feet have been trimmed. We're trying to fatten him up.' She kept her voice light, deliberately misunderstanding.

Holly giggled. 'I meant the bloke who rescued him!' She nudged Rachel. 'Come on, spill. I've wondered about him loads since he came to the surgery.'

'Who is this mystery man?' Nell said. 'He's obviously made a big impression on you all. Why?'

'I was wondering that myself,' Izzy said.

Briefly, Anna explained about his strange attire, his sunglasses and his hunched posture. 'Of course, it makes sense now. He was wearing sunglasses to hide his black eye, and he was probably in a bit of a state anyway, because he wanted to get to Folly Farm to check on Fred and sort out some food and water for him. No mystery at all, really.'

'Except . . . ' Holly glanced around at them all. 'I still think there's something familiar about him. Don't you?'

Anna and Rachel shrugged, looking blank.

'No.' Anna sounded thoughtful. 'I don't think he's from the village. He certainly doesn't ring any bells with me.'

'And he said he holidayed in the village once, years ago,' Rachel added, 'so he's definitely not local.'

'What's his name?'

'Alexander South,' Holly said promptly.

'He likes to be called Xander,' Rachel added.

It was Nell's turn to sound thoughtful. 'That's tugging at my memory,' she admitted. 'There's something . . . ' She shrugged. 'Sorry, can't think. So,' she said, smiling suddenly, 'what does he look like? Good boyfriend material?'

Rachel felt a chill and shivered. 'Never really took much notice,' she lied. 'Just your average bloke. Nothing much to say.'

It was as she had feared. Despite her best efforts, the conversation was leading back to men, relationships, and, no doubt, the fact that she and Holly were the only two single women in the group. They would be trying to fix her up with Xander South before she knew it, and that would never happen. Even if he'd seemed keen on her, which he hadn't, she would never go down that road again. Especially not with someone who cheerfully admitted that he was no stranger to fighting. She had no interest in any man, let alone someone like that, and Sam was going nowhere near him. She would make damn sure of it.

* * *

Xander leaned back in the battered old armchair, experiencing an unfamiliar feeling of contentment. Escaping to Bramblewick had, he realised, been the right move after all.

He had no idea why the place had popped into his mind that day, just four weeks ago. Staring into the mirror in his trailer, barely recognising his own reflection, he'd pulled a face at hearing the usual chaos outside. He'd known then that he had to get away — far away. He just had to survive the next two weeks, then he could go — but to where?

It wasn't as easy as it sounded. There were so few places he could hide these days. It occurred to him to visit one of his friends in Australia, but he couldn't be bothered to go all that way. He was sick of America. It just reminded him of work, which was all he ever seemed to do over there. There was always Italy, or perhaps Greece; but truthfully, he didn't want to go abroad. He just wanted to go somewhere quiet, rural, picturesque. Somewhere he could take his dogs, chill out, and forget all about Lord Bay Curtis.

As Mrs Frost handed him a mug of hot chocolate, he reflected how the image of Bramblewick had appeared before him, like a mirage in the desert — a long-distant memory of pretty stone cottages, a fast-flowing stream with a cute bridge, and a farm where his grandad used to take him to buy eggs. He'd remembered, with a sudden sharp clarity, the stunning beauty of the North York Moors which surrounded the village, the sheep that wandered the green, the ancient church that sat in the heart of the village, and the cosy pub that he and his grandparents had eaten in a couple of times, tucking in to roast beef and Yorkshire pudding, even though it was a very hot summer, because *you can't go to Yorkshire and not eat the Yorkshire puds*. He'd smiled to himself, remembering his grandad's insistence, and how their eyes had widened at the sizes of the portions on the plates.

Seeing the change in his reflection that day, as he remembered that childhood holiday, had surprised him. His expression had completely altered. He couldn't remember the last time he'd looked that happy. If just the memory of Bramblewick could cheer him up like that, what would a holiday there achieve?

Now, as he tentatively took a sip of the hot chocolate in the informal sitting room of Folly Farm, he realised it was like coming home. He was happy. He'd fallen in love with the village all over again, and the thought of going back to work was filling him with dread.

He thought about the four missed calls on his mobile. Penny wasn't going to let it drop, he realised. 'It's all very well playing hard to get,' she told him, 'but you're pushing it. You're being a fool. Come back to London and do as you're told, for goodness' sake.'

His response had been to hang up — which wasn't very mature of him, he admitted ruefully. He just hadn't known what else to say. Penny wasn't the sort of person to understand how he felt, and she definitely wouldn't feel any empathy with his desire to stay in Bramblewick. As much as he loved her, they were very different people. She was all sharp suits and sleek hair, a mobile phone permanently glued to one ear, a planner clutched in one hand. She knew people, she knew the business, and she knew what she wanted — for herself and for him. He couldn't blame her for not understanding. Once, they'd been on the same page. He'd been as driven as she was — maybe more so. Sometimes, he thought, you had to be careful what you wished for.

'What's this one called again?' Sam's voice cut through his thoughts, and he smiled down at the tawny-haired boy who was sitting on the floor, his arm around the youngest of the miniature poodles.

'That one's Belle,' he said, nodding at the red three-year-old, 'and that one,' he added, indicating the four-year-old black poodle, 'is Rumpel.'

'I must say,' Mrs Frost said, 'I never thought poodles could look so — you know — normal.'

'Normal?' Xander raised an eyebrow. 'What do you mean?'

'You know,' she said, 'like proper dogs. Not walking pompoms.'

He laughed. 'Their hair doesn't grow in that shape, you know. You have to clip them to achieve it. We preferred the more natural look. They still need clipping regularly, but we clip them evenly all over.'

'Who's 'we'?' Mrs Frost gave him a wide smile. 'Got a nice girlfriend tucked away, have you? Is she in Bramblewick too?'

Xander shook his head. 'They belonged to an ex-girlfriend. She got them because she thought they would make cute accessories. Unfortunately, she picked miniature poodles instead of toy, and they got too big for her taste. Unfortunately for her, that is. Lucky escape for them.' He sighed. 'I wish people would put more thought into buying dogs. Or any animal, come to that,' he added, thinking of Fred. 'Anyway, she got fed up with them and it was always me who ended up caring for them, so when we split up I asked if I could have them. Luckily, she was only too happy to offload them. They've been with me ever since.'

'Thought they were an odd choice for a fella,' she said, nodding sagely. 'I mean, no bloke would buy a poodle, would he?' She laughed suddenly. 'Trying to picture my husband with a poodle at his heels. No chance. He'd have been mortified.'

'That's a very sexist remark,' Xander told her sternly. 'Like saying a woman can't have a Rottweiler or a German Shepherd. I'll have you know, poodles are very friendly, intelligent and affectionate dogs. I'm extremely fond of them both.'

'Ah, but would you have chosen to

buy a poodle yourself?' she said slyly.

Xander hesitated. 'No. I suppose I wouldn't,' he admitted eventually, tutting good-humouredly as she laughed.

'Well, I'm glad your girlfriend was horrible,' Sam said cheerfully. 'I wouldn't have met Belle and Rumpel otherwise.'

'She wasn't horrible,' Xander assured him. 'Just had some funny ideas sometimes. We parted as friends.'

'That's very good to hear,' Mrs Frost said. 'Too many couples split up these days, and when they do it gets very acrimonious.' She looked across at Sam, who was happily teaching Belle to walk on two legs, like a little circus dog. Xander didn't miss the look of anxiety on her face, though she quickly smiled as she looked back at him. He wondered what had gone on between Rachel and her child's father, but dismissed the thought. It was none of his business.

At the sound of the back door opening, his heart sank a little.

'Rachel?' Mrs Frost sounded questioning, although who else she'd be expecting, Xander wasn't sure. As the living room door was pushed open, he found himself staring up into Rachel's eyes almost defiantly, sure she'd disapprove of his presence.

She looked flushed, her dark eyes bright. She'd definitely had a drink or two.

'Did you get a taxi, love?' Mrs Frost jumped up, rushing to remove her daughter's coat as if she were a small child, rather than a grown woman.

Rachel shook her head. 'Walked.' She turned to watch Sam, who was now showing Rumpel how to roll over — at least, Xander thought with a grin, he thought he was. Those dogs were already trained to do everything Sam was now intent on teaching them. 'Having fun, Sam?'

Sam's face lit up. 'Aren't they lovely, Mum? Their names are Belle and Rumpel, and they're miniature poodles. They're ever so clever.'

Xander watched as a wide smile spread across Rachel's face, and she watched Sam with delight and — was that relief? He felt himself start to relax, and realised he'd tensed upon her arrival. Her evident disapproval of him had clearly unnerved him more than he'd acknowledged. Maybe it was good for him. People tended to fawn over him, tell him how wonderful he was. It was a refreshing change to have someone so clearly unimpressed with him, if a little deflating. It was character-building, he decided, forcing himself to smile warmly at her, although it felt as if he was asking for trouble.

Sure enough, as her glance fell on him, her smile died; and Xander felt something inside him curl up and die, too. How did she do that?

'I gather these are your dogs?'

'They are.' He realised he sounded defensive. She seemed to bring out the worst in him.

'Rachel, you're just in time for hot chocolate,' her mother said, hooking the coat over her arm. 'Sit yourself down and get warm in front of the fire. I'll heat up some milk.'

As Mrs Frost hurried into the kitchen, Rachel did as she was told, and Xander tried to ignore the childish voice in his head that was telling him how spoilt and pampered she was by her mother. She was a grown woman, for goodness' sake, but her mother seemed to run around after her as if she was still a teenager. Then he remembered how many people ran around after him, and his annoyance evaporated. He was being unreasonable. He knew nothing about her, or their relationship. Since when did he get so judgmental?

'What brings you here at this time of night?' Her voice was light, but he sensed an edge. She wasn't comfortable with him being at the farm.

'I was kind of restless,' he told her, matching her casual tone in spite of his underlying feelings. 'I thought I'd take some air, walk the dogs. Then I decided to come up and see Fred. I wasn't going to disturb your family, but

Rumpel here decided to have a conversation with Fred, and your mum came out to see what the noise was and invited us in.'

'She would,' Rachel murmured.

'She's a very kind and generous lady,' he retorted, trying to bite down the flash of irritation. What had he ever done to her to make her so hostile?

'They're so cute, aren't they, Mum?' Sam said, evidently not noticing the tension in the room. 'Can we have a dog?'

Rachel's smile was tight. 'I think we have enough on our hands with a horse, don't you?'

Ouch! Another barbed comment. Xander sighed, feeling out of his depth. The plain fact was, this was all new to him. Being so obviously unwanted was unfamiliar territory, and although he'd craved normality for a long time, now it was here, it was proving to be deeply uncomfortable. He'd been in his privileged bubble for far too long, he realised. He'd prided himself on not falling for the hype. Now it occurred to him that he'd not been as clever as he'd supposed, nor so immune to flattery as he'd convinced himself he was. Maybe, he thought, Rachel was exactly what he needed. Maybe it was worth the discomfort if it woke him up and made him live in the real world again.

'But Fred doesn't take any looking after, does he?' Sam persisted. 'I'd love to have a dog in the house, so I could play with him and feed him and take him for walks.'

Seeing Rachel's set mouth, Xander had a feeling Sam was wasting his time. Evidently, Sam realised it too. He pursed his lips and folded his arms sulkily. 'Why don't you like animals? Dad always said I could have a dog, but *you* would never let me get one.'

Xander watched, surprised, as Rachel's whole demeanour changed. Her face took on a wounded expression, her eyes were full of anxiety, and she wrapped her arms around herself, as if protecting herself from something. 'It wouldn't have been fair,' she began, and he noted the strained tone of her voice, 'what with me and — and your dad being out at work all day, and you at school.'

'Well, Nanna's here all day,' Sam pointed out, 'so I don't see what your excuse is now.'

'This isn't our home, Sam,' Rachel said shakily. 'At least, not really. I mean — '

'You said it was!' he blurted out. 'You said we'd be staying here for good, and I had to get used to it. You made me go to that stupid new school and leave my friends behind because we had to live with Nanna — so is it our home, or isn't it?'

Rachel looked completely out of her depth. Xander was intrigued at the change in her, but also overwhelmed with a sudden pity for her. Something was clearly upsetting her. In spite of their prickly relationship, he felt obliged to step in to try to help.

'I think what your mum is trying to say is that, although this is your home, it really belongs to your nan, so it's not up to your mum to say whether or not you can have a dog.' It was the best he could do, given his complete ignorance of what was really going on with this family.

Rachel closed her eyes as Sam said, 'Nanna wouldn't mind. She's been really happy to see the dogs tonight, and she loves having Fred on the farm. It's just you, being awkward. You always spoil everything, Dad said — '

Rachel jumped up and rushed out of the room, leaving Xander staring after her in surprise. He turned slowly to Sam, who looked a bit shamefaced. 'Well, she does,' he muttered sulkily, stroking Rumpel's black ears. 'Dad always says she takes the fun out of everything.'

Xander shuffled awkwardly, not sure how to respond. He really didn't want to get involved in what was clearly a complicated situation. 'Mums have a very tough time of it,' he said, trying to sound cheery. 'Hard enough looking after a family without being a nurse too. That's a very important job.'

'Not as important as my dad's job,' Sam said, sounding mutinous. 'He's in charge of other people's money, and he's ever so clever. You should see his car. It's well cool.' He sighed and glanced around the living room. 'And our house is really big, and my bedroom's got Marvel wallpaper, and I got a new bike at Christmas but it's still at home and I don't know when I'll get to go back there. Mum keeps saying soon, but it never happens.'

He stared into Rumpel's eyes and the dog returned the look, tilting his head to one side as if trying to understand. Xander realised, suddenly, that he was doing exactly the same and straightened his head immediately. 'I'm sure things will get sorted out, one way or the other,' he murmured, not sure what he could say to reassure the boy. It must be tough for him, leaving his dad and his home behind, but who knew what had gone on to cause the split between Sam's parents? It wasn't any of Xander's business, and he didn't want to say the wrong thing and make matters worse. 'I'd better be going,' he said, deciding he'd more than outstayed his welcome.

Sam looked up, evidently disappointed. 'Do you have to go?'

Xander smiled as he pulled on his jacket. 'Afraid so. Have you seen the time? You should have been in bed ages ago.'

'Will you bring the dogs to see me again?' Sam demanded.

'Of course, if it's okay with your mum and nan,' Xander promised, not certain that permission would be forthcoming from Rachel at least. He collected the leads from the coffee table and clipped them to the dogs' collars. Sam sighed and flopped onto the sofa. 'I'll pop by and see Fred tomorrow,' Xander added. 'Might see you then? At least it's Saturday, so no school.'

Sam cheered up. 'Cool. I'll see you tomorrow. If I'm not in the yard, you will knock and let me know you're here?'

'I will,' Xander said. 'See you, Sam.'

'See you, Xander.'

Rachel and her mum were huddled together as he went through to the kitchen. Rachel looked upset, and Mrs Frost had her arm around her. They moved apart as he appeared, and he moved awkwardly towards the back door, pulling two very curious poodles who were clearly dying to stop and investigate the situation more closely.

'I'll be off, then,' he said, trying to sound casual. 'Thanks very much for the hot chocolate and the warm welcome, Mrs Frost. Very kind of you.'

'Oh, Xander, I've told you, call me Janie,' she said, waving a hand at him. 'You take care of yourself on those roads in the dark.'

He gave her a crooked grin. 'I will.' He nodded awkwardly at Rachel. 'Goodnight.'

She nodded back, not speaking, and he pulled open the back door, leading the dogs into the yard. As he headed towards his car, he heard the door open again, and stopped as he felt a hand on his arm. Spinning round, he was surprised to see it was Rachel. It was too dark to make out her expression, but her voice was shaky as she spoke to him.

'I'd appreciate it if you kept away from Sam,' she told him.

'I'm sorry?'

'I understand you have to come here to see Fred, but I'd prefer it if you came when Sam's at school.'

He frowned. 'Have I done something wrong?'

She'd wrapped her arms around herself again and was shivering. 'I just — I don't know you. You must surely see that it's not appropriate for you to spend time with my son?'

He felt a surge of anger and fought to push it down. 'What are you insinuating?'

'I'm not insinuating anything. I'm just protecting my child. Nothing wrong with that, is there?'

'Of course not, but I'm — ' He stopped and shook his head. 'If that's what you want.'

'It is.' She hesitated. 'I don't know you, or anything about you. You could be anyone. All I know is, you're a man who admits he likes a fight. I don't think you're the sort of person who should be spending time with an impressionable child.'

Xander stared at her incredulously. 'Who said I like a fight?'

'You did. You said that wasn't your first black eye, and that implies — '

'Rachel, you've got me all wrong. You really have.'

'Have I?' Her tone was challenging, and he knew she didn't really believe it. The thing was, to put her right, he would have to tell her the truth about himself, and he realised that he didn't want to do that. It was refreshing being no one important, being anonymous. He was relishing the privacy, the lack of pressure. He wasn't ready to give that up — not yet.

'Yes, you have,' he said with a sigh. 'But I guess you'll never believe that, so I'll leave you to it. Will you tell Sam I'm sorry about tomorrow?'

'Tomorrow?'

'I promised I'd bring the dogs round tomorrow, since he's not at school.'

'Oh.' She shivered again. 'That's awkward.'

'It is.' He wanted to take off his jacket and wrap it around her shoulders, but he had a feeling she wouldn't appreciate the gesture. 'I'm sorry. I should have checked with you first.'

'Yes, you should.' She rubbed her forehead, sounding weary. 'Okay, if you promised him, then you can pop round, just for half an hour or so. But don't make him any more promises, all right?'

'Fair enough,' he said.

She nodded. 'Thank you.'

As she turned to go back inside, he murmured, 'Goodnight, Rachel.'

She stopped for a moment but didn't look round. 'Night.'

Xander watched her as she hurried back to the farmhouse, then led his excited dogs back to the car, thinking that Rachel was one heck of a puzzle

— and realising, with a sudden pang of anxiety, that he was quite interested in working that puzzle out.

5

'The village is full of it!' Holly sounded as if she was about to burst with excitement. 'Loads of people were talking about it in Maudie's when I popped in for a loaf for Lulu.' She turned to Rachel, her eyes wide. 'Didn't I say his face was familiar? Fancy, a famous actor in Bramblewick!'

Riley and Connor were standing by Anna's desk, going through the list of visits. They nudged each other and grinned. 'Sounds like someone's star-struck,' Riley said, in his soft Scottish burr. 'Who is this famous actor you're all discussing?'

'Xander North! Can you believe it?'

Connor and Riley laughed. 'Never heard of him,' Connor admitted.

Holly didn't appear to notice. 'He was *actually* in our surgery. Rachel's *actually* met him, face-to-face, three times now. He registered here as Alexander South, which is apparently his real name, and I didn't click on, but Nell said the name was familiar when Rachel mentioned he liked to be called Xander, and no wonder. She's a huge fan of the show, and you should have heard her squeal when I rang up to tell her earlier.'

Riley frowned, clearly not finding it all so funny anymore. 'Who is this fella?'

Rachel shrugged, not much more clued up than he appeared to be. She'd been pretty shocked when Holly had excitedly informed her that the village was agog with the news that the star of one of the biggest series on television was staying in Sweet Briar Cottage, of all places. He'd made the mistake of going into Maudie's shop without his sunglasses, and had been spotted by local woman Laura Steele — who, unfortunately for Xander, was a huge television addict, and had recognised him immediately. The gossip had spread like wildfire.

Rachel didn't watch much television, and when she did she tended to stick to situation comedies. Real life was grim enough. She liked her viewing to be pure escapism.

Holly, however, seemed to know all about Lord Bay Curtis, the character played by Xander in his award-winning drama series, *Lord Curtis Investigates*. 'It's on Netflix. You must have seen it?'

'I don't have Netflix,' Riley announced, and Connor and Rachel both admitted that they hadn't either.

Holly looked incredulous. 'What century are you lot from? Even Lulu's got Netflix, and she's about a hundred!'

'Who's Lulu?' Rachel queried.

'Louisa Drake, one of our patients,' Anna explained. 'Holly's next-door neighbour.'

'Like my honorary gran, is Lulu,' Holly said, 'and she's proper down with the kids. Totally addicted to *Orange is the New Black*, I'll tell you. But Xander plays this gorgeous earl in the olden days, who lives in this amazing country estate, and he's a right charmer. You know, got women falling over themselves to hook him, 'cause he's quite a catch is Lord Curtis, obvs. Anyway, what they don't know is that, Lord Curtis is a secret crime fighter, and he's always doing investigations and stuff; which is a good job, because every woman he meets is either a victim or a murderer or a thief or something, so he's always either bringing them to justice or rescuing them. He's a dab hand with a pistol, and he's ever so handy with his sword.'

'I'll bet he is,' Rachel murmured, rolling her eyes.

'Seriously, it's ever so good. And the thing is, he tries to be nice to all these wannabe countesses, but his heart belongs to Lady Constance. Except she's a secret jewel thief, so he won't marry her, even though he loves her so much, but he won't give her away either, so he's always battling his conscience. She pops up two or three times each series. Ooh, I'll tell who she's played by — that woman who used to be in *Corrie* a few years ago. What's her name? You know, she did that coffee commercial, too. Her with the black hair and the eyebrows. Oh!' Obviously registering their blank expressions, she tutted impatiently. 'I don't know why any of you lot have a television licence.'

'I've often thought the same myself,' Riley agreed.

'Sorry, Holls, but Gracie likes to watch her DVDs, and by the time we've got her to bed we can't be bothered to watch television,' Anna said, patting Holly on the shoulder. 'I'm sure it's a very good programme.'

'Oh, it is. And it's ever so popular. Especially in America. They love him over there — probably the whole aristocracy and stately home thing. Xander's won lots of awards, and he's often in America doing publicity tours, and — oh!' She gripped Anna's arm. 'I've just remembered! He used to be engaged to that redhead. You know the one! She was up for a Golden Globe the other year for that film about the travelling fair that was a cover for — ' She broke off, shaking her head. 'You haven't a clue who I'm talking about, have you? You know her. She did that perfume ad the other Christmas, and we got sick of seeing her.'

'Hmm. Vaguely remember her,' Anna said. 'So, he's not engaged now?'

'No, they broke it off. It was all very amicable apparently. At least,' she nodded shrewdly, 'that's what they tell us.'

Rachel thought about the poodles, and wondered if it was the redheaded actress who had once owned them. She could hardly believe that she'd had an acting superstar in her living room — well, her mum's living room. Her mother would be thrilled to bits.

'Seems like he's a hero onscreen and off,' Connor said dryly, 'seeing as he's into rescuing horses in his spare time.'

'Gosh, and you're looking after Fred for him,' Holly breathed. 'I'm so jealous of you, Rachel! Could you get me an autograph? Ooh, even better, do you think you could get him to meet up with us one evening in the pub? That would be amazing.'

'We're hardly best friends,' Rachel said, feeling cornered. She could hardly explain that she'd been rude and unwelcoming to Holly's heartthrob, could she? But so what if he was a famous actor? It made no difference to how she felt. She didn't want him anywhere near Sam. In fact, since he seemed to be famous for rescuing stupid women, or falling in love with or capturing evil ones, she was even more certain that she wanted him to stay away from her son. The last thing Sam needed was to be around someone so chauvinistic.

'You're his horse's landlady, so you're practically family,' Holly protested.

'Right, we're off on our visits now,' Connor said, dropping a kiss on Anna's cheek. 'Should be back in time to grab a quick sandwich before afternoon surgery, judging by this little lot,' he added, nodding at the pile of patient notes in his hand. 'Seems everyone's decided to get sick today.'

'See you later,' Anna said, smiling. 'Have you finished your surgery, Rachel?'

Rachel nodded. 'Just going to pop home for lunch and see how Mum's doing.'

'Great,' Holly said, folding her arms. 'Ignore the fact that we have a superstar in our community. Let's just carry on as normal.'

'That,' said Anna with a grin, 'is exactly what we plan to do. Cheer up, Holls. I've got a wonderful afternoon planned for you.'

'Oh?' Holly raised an eyebrow. 'Doing what?'

Anna handed her a couple of sheets of paper. 'Going through that little lot. Smoking statuses need doing before the end of the month, so you can ring all these patients and find out if they're smokers or non-smokers.'

'And how many they smoke a day,' added Connor.

They all looked at each other, their faces bright with amusement, and chorused, 'Five!' It was the stock answer that most patients gave them.

Holly sighed. 'All right. Who needs Hollywood actors when you've got a glamorous job like this?'

Rachel patted her on the shoulder, then headed out to the car park. Nursing might not be a glamorous job, she thought, but it was real. She'd rather hang out with normal villagers, many of whom didn't have two pennies to rub together, than all the Hollywood glitterati. Xander North, or Alexander South, or whoever he was in reality, had become even less desirable in her book. The one thing she was certain of was that she didn't want or need yet another actor in her life.

6

Rachel turned off her computer, removed her NHS smartcard from its slot in the keyboard, and grabbed her handbag from under the desk. It had been a busy morning. With more patients coming to the Bramblewick surgery from the surrounding villages, now that they were up to two GPs and a full-time nurse again, her clinics were always full. It felt as if she'd tackled everything that morning, from removing stitches to carrying out a diabetes review to doing an asthma check-up. At least, she thought ruefully, it was never boring. In spite of it all, she loved her job, and she loved being back in Bramblewick. She just wished she hadn't waited so long to come home.

Then again, she realised, as she rummaged in her handbag for her car keys, the timing had never been right before. This branch surgery had been too small to support a full-time nurse until Connor had arrived and things had started to change. After the previous GP — Anna's father — had passed away, the main Castle Street surgery in Helmston had considered closing down Bramblewick, but Connor had led a protest and put in place a plan of action to expand it instead. The changes in government funding had also made the bosses at the main surgery think again, and they'd altered their plans. Riley MacDonald, a GP based at Castle Street, had made the decision to move to the branch surgery and join Connor, and the practice manager and partners had agreed to a full-time practice nurse for Bramblewick too.

Building work would be starting any day on the extension that was being carried out on the surgery. There was going to be a new consulting room for a third GP, and the waiting room was to be expanded and new toilet facilities created. There would also be more room in the main office, with a designated area for a kitchenette, complete with dining table. Rachel's marriage had collapsed at just the right time, it seemed.

Except — except it hadn't really collapsed a few weeks ago at all. Rachel paused in her search for her keys and stared at the dark computer screen, as if seeing her relationship playing out before her eyes. It had died years ago, when Sam was just a baby and she'd realised what a cruel man her husband really was. Why hadn't she left then? She'd asked herself that question so many times and had cursed herself for her own cowardice. She'd made so many excuses: she didn't want to worry her parents; she didn't have anywhere to go; she couldn't afford to be a single mum, and she wouldn't be able to work full-time with a small child to care for; she didn't want Sam to grow up without a father. Rachel tutted. Growing up without a father was infinitely preferable to growing up with the wrong sort of father, and she was very much afraid that was what Sam had been doing for far too long. She only hoped she hadn't left it too late.

Connor and Riley were just leaving to carry out their visits when she walked into the main office. They waved at her then headed out of the door, medical bags in hand, deep in discussion about some football team's latest dismal performance.

Holly was tucking into a cheese sandwich. She frowned as Rachel grabbed her coat from the rack near the door. 'You off home again? Why don't you ever have your lunch here? It's a proper hike up to Folly Farm. By the time you get there, it must be nearly time to come home again.'

'Hardly.' Rachel grinned. 'Besides, who wants to sit here and watch you stuff your face? Fred has better eating manners than you.'

'Charming!' Holly tutted, waving her half-eaten sandwich in protest.

Anna laughed. 'She's got a point, though. Is that your phone ringing, Rachel?'

Realising it was indeed her ringtone, Rachel rummaged in her handbag and brought out her mobile. Seeing the name on the screen, her stomach churned in dread. 'It's the school.'

Anna sat down beside Holly, and they watched quietly as Rachel listened to the person on the phone. It was the headmistress. Rachel nodded tensely and informed her she'd be at the school within minutes.

'What's happened? Is Sam okay?' Anna gave her a sympathetic look.

'I'm — I'm not sure. There's been some sort of incident in the dinner hall. I have to go.' She shrugged on her coat, her face tight with worry.

'Do you want me to ring your mum? She'll be expecting you, won't she?'

'Oh, please, Anna,' Rachel said gratefully. 'That would be so good of you. Tell her not to worry and I'll grab something to eat from Nell's. Tell her I'll call her when I know Sam's okay.'

'Will do. Try not to worry too much, okay? I'm sure Sam's not hurt.'

As Rachel hurried out of the office, she wondered how she could ever confess to someone like Anna — or to anyone, come to that — that it wasn't Sam she was worried about.

⋆　⋆　⋆

Mrs Morgan motioned to Rachel to sit down. The headmistress's eyes were kind, and there was no note of condemnation in her voice as she explained what had happened in the lunch hall. She simply sounded concerned, and a little bit puzzled, which wasn't surprising.

'It seemed to come out of the blue,' she told Rachel. 'There had been a bit of bickering and some pushing in the queue, but that's fairly standard. It was certainly nothing to give us concern. Miss Lewis, who was standing close by, saw and heard the whole thing, and she said the worrying thing was that Sam's temper seemed to flare up out of nowhere.'

Miss Lewis, a fairly young teacher

with reddish-brown curls and large glasses, nodded in agreement. 'It was all good-natured at first. The boys often take the mickey out of each other, and there's a lot of light-hearted banter in the lunchtime queues, but Sam seemed to suddenly take offence at something one of the boys said. He started pushing the boy, Toby, and yelling at him to have more respect. Before I could intervene, he'd pushed Toby so strongly that the poor little lad went flying. I had to hold Sam back, because it looked as if he was about to jump on the boy and continue his attack. It was all a bit unnerving, to be honest.'

Rachel felt sick. That word! *Respect.* How many times had she been warned to have more respect for Grant? How many times had Sam heard it? She stared at Miss Lewis, feeling wretched. 'I'm so sorry. I — I don't know what to say.'

'Has this happened before, Mrs Johnson? Has Sam displayed any signs of aggression at his previous school?'

Rachel swallowed. 'I'm afraid he has. Only in the last few months,' she added hastily. 'He was perfectly fine before then. Unfortunately, he got into a fight with another boy during his last term at the school, and then there was an incident . . . ' She took a deep breath. 'He was making fun of a child who'd just started wearing glasses. The little boy retaliated, mocking something about Sam; so Sam punched him, then stamped on the glasses and broke them. It was awful, and so unlike him.'

She didn't miss the look the two women exchanged, but she could hardly blame them. They must be wondering what sort of boy they'd taken on.

'I do understand that Sam has been through a difficult time recently,' Mrs Morgan said. 'Your recent separation from his father and the move up here to North Yorkshire must have been quite an upheaval for him. You say his behaviour has only changed in the last few months? If that's the case, it could simply be down to the changes and the stress he's experienced. I'll expect him to apologise to the little boy he attacked, and I'll inform his teacher.'

So Izzy would know! Well, of course she would. How could she not be told?

'We'll be monitoring his conduct carefully. I'm sure you understand that we can't and won't tolerate bullying in this school.' She gave Rachel a sympathetic smile. 'It might perhaps be worth considering getting Sam some sort of counselling. Have you thought about that?'

Rachel bit her lip. 'I did think about it, yes. Perhaps I should consider it more seriously.'

'It might help him to adjust to everything that's happened to him in recent months.' Mrs Morgan glanced up at Miss Lewis. 'Could you show the boys in, please?'

Miss Lewis nodded, and Rachel took a deep breath as the door opened and the teacher ushered in Sam, alongside a freckle-faced boy with spiky, dark hair.

Rachel stared at her son, who stuck his hands in his pockets and looked away from her, only the reddening of his cheeks showing that he knew only too well that he was in trouble.

'Well, Sam, I've spoken to your mum about what happened. Is there anything you'd like to say?'

Sam looked mutinous. He shrugged. Rachel was mortified. *Show some remorse, for goodness' sake!*

The other boy glanced up at the headmistress. 'It's all right. He's said sorry to me, and we're friends again, aren't we, Sam?'

Sam looked at him and nodded. 'Yes, we are.'

'I'd like to hear you say you're sorry, and I'm sure your mum would like to hear it, too.'

Sam looked pretty fed up at being asked to apologise yet again, but he gave a big sigh and said, 'I'm sorry I pushed you, Toby.'

'S'okay.'

They grinned at each other, and

Rachel gave an inward sigh of relief.

'Well, in that case, we'll leave it at that,' Mrs Morgan said. 'But if this sort of thing happens again, Sam, you'll be in serious trouble. Do you understand that?'

'Yes, Mrs Morgan.'

'And I expect you have something to say to your mum, who's had to leave work to come all the way to the school to sort this out.'

Sam's eyes met Rachel's. She saw the shame in them, and felt some weird sort of hope. 'Sorry, Mum.'

Rachel nodded. 'All right, Sam. We'll talk more about this tonight when I get home.'

He looked less than thrilled at that prospect, but said nothing, following Miss Lewis and Toby out of the office.

Mrs Morgan looked at Rachel. 'Thank you for coming so promptly, Mrs Johnson, and thank you for your support. I'm sure Sam is a good boy at heart, and, hopefully we won't have a repeat of this behaviour. Have a think about the counselling. I know it's a big step to take, but Sam has been through a lot of upheaval, and who knows what effect it's had on him?' She stood and held out her hand to Rachel. 'Hopefully we won't have to call you in here again, unless it's in happier circumstances.'

Rachel shook her hand and left the office, feeling quite dazed. It felt as if all her worst fears were coming true. Why had she waited so long to leave Grant? She'd thought she and Sam had made their escape, but it seemed he was still influencing their lives, still influencing Sam. Maybe she'd left it too late after all.

7

It had been a tense meal at Folly Farm, as Rachel picked at her chicken casserole and Sam looked thoroughly miserable. Mrs Frost had been given the gist of what happened at the school, and was trying valiantly to jolly things along. 'How about a nice walk around the village? It's a lot warmer this evening. Seems a shame to be stuck in. What do you say, Sam?'

Sam shrugged. 'Not bothered.'

'Rachel?'

Rachel pushed her plate away and sighed. 'If you like.'

Her mother smiled brightly. 'Great. That's settled, then. Let's get ready. We'll worry about the pots when we get home.'

The streets of Bramblewick were quiet as they finally left the moors road behind them and entered the village centre. All the shops were in darkness, with only The Bay Horse lit up. They could hear the gurgling of the beck that cut through the village, and stopped for a moment to peer into its inky black depths.

'What about popping into the pub for a drink?' Mrs Frost suggested. 'They do a smashing hot chocolate, Sam. What do you think?'

Sam smiled for the first time all evening. 'Cool. Do they do marshmallows and whipped cream?'

'They do.'

He looked at Rachel. 'Can we, Mum?'

In spite of everything that had happened, Rachel found herself smiling at him, and reached over to ruffle his hair. 'Why not? We could do with a nice hot drink, and it will be a relief to get out of this chilly wind, whatever your nan said about it being warm tonight.'

Sam beamed at her and put his arms around her, and she held him to her, bursting with love for her little boy. Her mother's eyes glittered with unshed tears. 'Come on then, race you to the pub,' she said.

Sam was off and halfway there before they had chance to even think about it. Rachel looked at her mum and laughed.

'He'll be all right, Rachel. Don't worry yourself. It's just a blip. We both know Sam's a good boy, don't we?'

Half-tempted to tell her of her fears, Rachel merely nodded and slipped her arm through her mum's. 'Come on. There's a big mug of hot chocolate with my name on it.'

The pub was warm, cosy and cheerful, and within ten minutes they were sitting at a table, sipping hot chocolate and laughing at each other for wearing whipped cream moustaches. Rachel was just beginning to relax when her mother suddenly nudged her.

'Look, over there! It's Xander.'

Rachel felt a flutter of irritation and glanced around, eventually spotting him sitting alone, nursing a pint of beer in a corner of the bar.

Sam's eyes sparkled with sudden excitement. 'Can we sit with him?'

Rachel shook her head. 'He might want to be alone, Sam. You can't just dump yourself on someone else. For all we know he doesn't want any company.'

'Oh rubbish.' Mrs Frost tutted, dismissing Rachel's words out of hand. Sometimes, Rachel reflected, her mother could be extremely frustrating. 'Xander's a sociable sort of chap. He must want company, or he wouldn't have come in here, would he? He'd be at home — especially since he knows everyone is very aware of who he is now. I'll invite him over.'

Before Rachel could stop her, she'd made her way over to Xander.

Rachel's face burned as he glanced over at her and Sam. She saw his expression as he watched her, clearly uncertain that he'd be welcome at their table. She felt suddenly ashamed of herself. In spite of her misgivings, she gave him a half-smile and nodded. Xander picked up his pint and followed her mother back.

'Isn't it lovely to see Xander again?' Her mum sat down, looking far too pleased with herself. 'It seems like ages since you came up to the farm. What have you been doing?'

Xander didn't look at Rachel, who was grateful that he didn't give her away. He'd kept his promise, staying only half an hour during his last visit and not coming up to Folly Farm since. 'Sorry. I've been a bit busy. How is Fred?'

'Oh, he's doing fine. Did the vet send you the bill for his treatment?'

'He did, and so did the farrier.'

'You must come and see Fred soon,' Mrs Frost reproached him. 'He's your horse now, after all.'

Xander glanced at Rachel. 'I'd like to,' he said slowly.

Rachel gave a tight smile. 'Of course you must come and see him,' she said, and took a gulp of her hot chocolate.

Xander said nothing but picked up her paper serviette and handed it to her. Guessing she'd got cream on her face, Rachel flushed and dabbed at her mouth, feeling awkward and embarrassed.

'Where are Belle and Rumpel?' Sam demanded.

Xander put down his pint. 'All tucked up in their bed, nice and warm at home. You can't bring dogs to a pub. You know — rules.' He rolled his eyes mockingly and Sam laughed.

'I wouldn't have thought you'd have come out somewhere so public,' Mrs Frost said. 'With all the gossip about your job, I thought you'd be hiding away from everyone.'

'I was at first,' he admitted. 'Then I thought, what's the point? They know where I am, and really, who cares? Once the initial excitement dies down, people tend to leave me alone. If I mix with the locals, get out and about in the village, they'll soon get used to me and forget all about it.'

'Very wise,' Mrs Frost said, nodding. 'I have to confess, I've never seen *Lord*

Curtis Investigates, but I did love you in that BBC drama you made a couple of years ago. The one where you played the alcoholic lawyer. You managed to make me feel quite sorry for him, even though I wanted to kick him up the bum at the same time.'

Xander's eyes widened. 'You knew who I was?'

Rachel was astonished. 'You never said.'

'Well — ' Her mother shrugged. ' — I thought that if you wanted me to know, you'd have mentioned it; and, as you didn't say a word, I figured it wasn't something you wished to discuss.' She turned eager eyes on him. 'You must come for tea one night, Xander — mustn't he, Rachel? Ooh, I know! Why not come for your Sunday dinner this weekend? We'd love to have you. Wouldn't we, Rachel?'

Rachel could feel Xander's eyes burning into hers. Sam was looking at her excitedly. What could she say? 'Er, yes. Sure. Why not?' Surely, after their little talk, he would refuse?

'I'd love to,' she heard him say, and she pursed her mouth crossly. She could hardly reproach him now, could she? And Sam would only resent her even more if she tried to take away his new buddy. As for her mother, she seemed to adore him. How annoying was that!

'Excuse me, I just need to . . . ' She stood and headed out of the bar towards the toilets. She needed to get away and calm down. She was feeling cornered and trapped, and panic was rising. How could she protect Sam when all around her were unsuitable men — men that Sam seemed all too keen to look up to?

A few minutes later, she splashed water onto her face and stared at her reflection in the mirror in the toilets. It had been a horrible day and she was feeling confused and unhappy. She had no idea what to do for the best. It felt as if there was no way out, nowhere to turn. Now she had to go back into the bar and sit at that table with Xander, seeing Sam and her mother fawning over him. She wanted to scream, really she did. It was all so unfair.

With a big sigh, she pulled open the door and stepped into the lobby, almost colliding with Xander, who, it appeared, had been waiting for her.

'It may have escaped your notice,' she said coldly, 'but these are the ladies' toilets. You'll find the — er — *gentlemen's* facilities down the corridor, if that's what you want.'

Xander frowned, his arms folded as he leaned against the door post. 'What I want, Rachel, is for you to tell me what it is, exactly, that I'm supposed to have done.'

'I don't know what you're talking about,' she said, tucking a wayward strand of hair behind her ear and trying to push past him.

His hand cupped her arm and she flinched unthinkingly. Immediately, he let go. 'Did I hurt you?'

She shook her head, annoyed with

herself. 'No. No, it's fine.'

'It clearly isn't fine.' He sighed. 'Look, Rachel, I'm not trying to push my way into your family, if that's what you're worried about; and I'm not trying to come on to you, either.'

She could feel her face turning pink with embarrassment. 'I never thought you were.'

'Really? Then what it is it? What have I done to make you so angry with me?'

She met his gaze and saw the genuine confusion in his eyes. Suddenly deflated, she rubbed her forehead and leaned against the wall, exhausted. 'Nothing. You haven't done anything, really.'

'Something about me clearly winds you up,' he said gently. 'If there's some misunderstanding, I'd really like to sort it out now.'

'It's just . . . ' She shrugged, not sure how far she wanted to go in her explanation. 'I suppose it was the black eye. What you said about it not being the first you've had.'

'That? That's not what it sounds like.'

'And this programme you're in. To be honest, this Lord Whatshisface sounds like a real creep. All that rescuing damsels in distress rubbish, and brandishing his sword, and lusting after some glamorous jewel thief.'

'You've watched it?'

Her face burned even hotter. 'Well, no,' she admitted. 'But I've heard all about it. Sounds pretty dismal to me.'

To her surprise and relief, he burst out laughing. 'It's not great,' he said. 'It has an awful lot of fans, though. Maybe you and I just have exceptionally good taste.'

Her eyebrows shot up. 'You don't like it either? So why do you do it then?'

'Money.' He shrugged. 'Sounds mercenary, and it is. I was a jobbing actor for years. Could barely meet my rent, never mind buy food or put money in the electricity meter. I was doing all sorts to earn cash, from delivering Chinese takeaways to washing cars to dog-walking. Yes, honestly. Then my agent got me an audition for this role. It sounded a bit naff to me, even then, but I was desperate, and pretty determined to get the part. I gave it everything I had — really turned on the charm.' He shook his head, smiling at the memory. 'When they told me the part of Lord Bay Curtis was mine, I couldn't believe it. Boy, did Penny and I celebrate that night!'

'Penny?'

'My agent. She's stood by me through thick and thin. She's not too happy with me at the moment, though.'

'Oh? Why's that?'

'There's an offer she wants me to take. A film.' He sighed. 'I've got the producer of *Lord Curtis Investigates* on my case, too. I was contracted for six series, and we've done those now, but the fans are clamouring for another. The producers are keen to deliver. I suppose I can't blame them, but I'm so over playing this guy. Heaven knows, I don't need the money any more, and there are other things I want to do, other offers on the table. Penny thinks I should ride the gravy train as long as I can, but . . . Anyway, the black eyes I was talking about — they were only due to fight routines and rehearsals gone wrong. Back in the early days, I really went for it. I've learned a lot since then. But I've never fought in my private life. I couldn't fight my way out of a paper bag, which is why I ended up with a black eye when I confronted Fred's owner. I'd love to say he came off worse, but he really didn't. I'm useless. Maybe I shouldn't have tried, but you have to admit that one time was forgivable, surely?'

She studied his face, looking for signs of deception, but he met her gaze unflinchingly, his expression open and honest. 'I'm sorry,' she said. 'I was just looking out for Sam. I don't want him to have any bad influences around him. It's hard enough being a parent to a young boy. The last thing I need is for him to look up to someone who enjoys fighting and getting into trouble, and has no respect whatsoever for women.'

She'd tried to keep the bitterness out of her voice, but wasn't entirely sure she'd succeeded, judging by the thoughtful look on his face.

He held out his hand to her. 'I totally understand that, but that person isn't me. How about we call a truce? Start again.'

Rachel hesitated, but couldn't think of a single fair reason to refuse his offer. Besides, her mum and Sam clearly liked him; and he *had* rescued Fred, after all. Maybe he was one of the good guys. Maybe she should give him a chance.

Her hand clasped his. 'Truce.'

Xander's eyes sparkled and his mouth curved into a wide smile. Rachel felt a sudden unexpected joy, seeing the happiness her reaction had given him.

'In that case,' he said, 'will you let me buy you a drink, so we can celebrate our new friendship?'

'Go on, then,' she said, realising she was smiling back at him. 'The hot chocolates are on you.'

8

Merlyn ran his hand down Fred's foreleg, then straightened, nodding in satisfaction. 'He's doing well. Looks like a different horse.' He laughed as Fred nudged him. 'Reckon you feel like a different horse too, eh, old chap?'

He smiled at Xander. 'Must have been pretty miserable for him, tethered on council wasteland. Much better for him to have the run of this field. There's only one thing he's lacking now.'

Xander frowned. 'Which is?'

'A companion. Horses are sociable animals. They like to have at least one friend with them. Any chance of that?' Seeing Xander's doubtful expression, he added, 'Doesn't have to be another horse. Lots of people I know put a donkey or a sheep in. I've got one particular client whose pony is quite besotted with a Rough Fell ewe.' He gave a deep hearty laugh. 'Was going to say, follows her around like a little lamb. There may be some truth in that.'

'I can see what you mean, but this isn't my land. I can hardly expect Mrs Frost — Janie — to take in yet another guest, can I?'

'Ah, I don't think Janie would mind. She's got a heart of gold, that woman. Between you and me, I haven't seen her looking this well since — well, since Jim passed.'

'Her husband?'

'That's right. Good man, Jim. We used to play darts together at The Swan Inn in Hatton-le-Dale.' He sighed, glancing behind him at the farmyard. 'Would you believe this used to be a thriving farm? Had a good herd of dairy cattle, and around three hundred sheep at one point.'

'What happened?'

'Foot-and-mouth.' Merlyn tutted. 'Back in 2001 it nearly wiped the industry out. Mind, to be fair, plenty of farms were already struggling. Cheap milk, cheap meat, cheap wool. Not much money to be made in any quarter, and when the disease struck — well, some decided it was the last straw.'

'Including Mr Frost?'

'Afraid so. He didn't see any point in struggling on. Janie wasn't a farming sort of woman. She'd grown up in Helmston and she worked there in a shop. As for Rachel, she had no intention of becoming a farmer. She was always set on being a nurse. So you see, Jim didn't think it worth fighting for any more. I could see his point, but I worried he'd go downhill after giving it up.'

'And did he?'

Merlyn shrugged, patting Fred's neck affectionately. 'When farming's in your blood, there's not a lot you can do to shift it. I reckon he missed it a lot more than he let on, but he made the best of things, the way people round here always do.' He shook his head. 'Funny thing is, I think Janie missed it, too. She'd never taken much of an active role on the farm, but she lost her spark when the herd went. It must have seemed like a ghost town here without the livestock. All that silence. All those empty outbuildings and fields.'

Xander was quiet, thinking about what Folly Farm had been like years ago, when his own grandfather had brought him to the house for eggs. He remembered chickens in the yard, and a distinctive smell in the air, and a general buzz of activity. He also had a vague memory of a smiling woman handing his grandad the eggs. She'd ruffled his hair. Had that been Janie? He felt a sudden sadness as he thought about the empty loose box he'd put Fred in that night. How bleak and desolate the farm had seemed. The heart had left Folly Farm.

'It's good to see her smiling again.' Merlyn sounded quite wistful. 'Always had a smile to light up the night skies, did Janie.' He tutted, suddenly brisk again. 'Anyway, have a think about it. Maybe put it to Janie? She might be more accommodating than you expect.'

'It's not that easy, though, is it? I'm not in Bramblewick permanently. I rented Sweet Briar Cottage until July, but after then — well, who knows? I won't be in this village, though, that's for sure. I can hardly expect Janie and Rachel to keep my animals here.' He rubbed the back of his neck thoughtfully. 'I really ought to be investigating livery for Fred. Trouble is, I'm not sure where I'll be, and I don't want him to be constantly moved around. Maybe I should look at a sanctuary.'

'Hmm. Maybe.' Merlyn picked up his bag. 'Well, if you're sure, although I think it would be a shame to take Fred away from his new family.' He gave Xander a sly look. 'Even Rachel seems quite fond of him. And Sam's so excited to have him around.'

'Rachel . . . ' Xander hesitated, not wishing to pry but longing to know more about her. Anything about her, really. 'She didn't live round here with her husband?'

'No. Somewhere near Leeds, I

believe. Met him at university.'

'Did you know him?'

'Never met him. Don't know if he ever visited. Suppose he must have, but I never saw him. I don't know anything about him, really, or their marriage, before you ask.'

'I wasn't going to ask,' Xander said hastily. 'None of my business.'

'No. Quite.' Merlyn grinned at him. 'Anyway, better get off. Got some sad business to deal with before lunch.' He glanced at his watch and pulled a face. 'Not looking forward to it.'

'Oh?' Xander followed him out of the field, closing the gate carefully behind him. 'What's happening?'

'Got to put an old chap to sleep.' Merlyn put his bag on the passenger seat of his Land Rover and climbed in. Winding down the window, he gave Xander a rueful look. 'His family are moving abroad. Emigrating. They can't take Duke with them, so they've asked me to take care of him, if you know what I mean.'

Xander was horrified. 'What! But you can't do that! Find him another home.'

'It's not that simple, Xander. Believe me, I've tried. Duke is fourteen, and he's got a heart condition. That's why they can't take him with them. He has cardiomyopathy, plus fluid on the lungs. To top it all, he had a minor stroke a couple of months ago, so he's on blood thinners for that, too. All told, his medication costs around a hundred and fifty pounds a month, and who's going to take on an old dog that costs so much to keep?'

'Wouldn't you give him a home?'

Merlyn smiled. 'Do you think I wasn't tempted? Truth is, Xander, if I took in every animal I wanted to save, I'd have no room left in the house. He's had a good life and a loving family. It's just a shame it has to end this way. I think he had a few months left in him, and he's not suffering. Quite a happy chap, actually. Just gets tired and tends to sleep a lot.'

'I'll take him.' Xander heard the

words coming out of his mouth before he'd even had time to process them.

Merlyn raised an eyebrow. 'You? But you just said yourself, you don't know where you'll be after July, and — '

'Wherever I am, I'll take care of him. Trust me on that. You can't just give up on him like that, after everything he's been through. His family must be feeling so guilty.'

Merlyn hesitated. 'They're struggling with it, I'll admit that, but I can't give them hope when you may not be the right man to take him on.'

'I'll pay for his medication, no problem.'

'I don't doubt that,' Merlyn said gently. 'But I'm thinking about your unsettled living arrangements and all the upheaval. Plus, you already have two dogs. How would they react to an old fellow in their midst? Would they bother him? Would they be too much for him to cope with?'

'Who are we talking about?' Janie had approached without either of them hearing her. She gave them both a broad grin. 'Sounds like an interesting conversation.'

Briefly, Xander filled her in about Duke. 'I suppose Merlyn's right,' he said grudgingly. 'Truth is, Mrs Lovelace, who owns the holiday cottage, probably wouldn't be happy with me taking on another dog. She only agreed to Belle and Rumpel because they were poodles and didn't shed hair.' He looked hopefully at Merlyn. 'I don't suppose this dog is a poodle?'

Merlyn laughed. 'No, afraid not. His father was a Heinz 57 — a bit of all sorts. His mother was Julian Twydale's best sheepdog. She was supposed to be mated with old Henry Parker's champion, but the rogue mongrel got there first.'

Janie's eyes widened, and she giggled. 'I remember that! Julian nearly had a fit when he found out she was already expecting. Aw, they were cute little puppies, weren't they? Think she had six, all told.'

'She did. Duke was the only one who stayed in the village.'

'I know Duke,' she said. 'The Carlyles bought him. He was the one who looked most like his mum, but Julian said he would never make a sheepdog. Aw, bless him. That it's come to this.' She shook her head. 'How time passes. Seems like only yesterday he was a little bundle of black-and-white fluff. Well,' she put her hands on her hips, 'he must come here, of course.'

Xander stared at her. 'Are you serious?'

'Of course. Poor old boy deserves a happy ending. He can see out his days in this farmhouse, with people who will care for him. And he knows us — well, he knows me. Me and Cassie Carlyle used to be in a reading group, and we went to each other's houses regularly, so I met him a few times. Haven't seen him for a year or so, but I'm sure he'll remember me.'

Merlyn pursed his lips, thinking. 'Are you sure about this, Janie? He may not have long left, you know. I mean, he's doing well at the moment with the tablets he's on, but I don't know how long it will last.'

'All the more reason to give him a happy life while I can,' she said firmly.

'And I'll pay for his medication, and any treatment or food he needs,' Xander said, turning to Merlyn, his eyes pleading. 'What do you say?'

'I'm about to go to the Carlyles now,' Merlyn said. 'I didn't want to put Duke through the final stress of going to the surgery, so I was going to do the deed at his home. I'll talk to them, see what they think. We have to weigh up whether the upheaval of going to a new home, losing his family, will be too much for him. I'm pretty certain they'll go for it, though. There have been a lot of tears these last few weeks, I'll tell you.'

Xander almost fell against the Land Rover with relief. 'Thanks, Merlyn. And you'll let us know as soon as you've asked?'

'You can count on it,' he promised, starting the engine. He turned a warm gaze on Janie. 'You're a rare woman, Janie.' He winked at them both. 'I'll be in touch very soon. Oh, and Xander, don't forget about that other matter. Worth some thought, eh?'

'What other matter?' Janie asked, as they waved Merlyn off.

Xander shrugged. 'Nothing important.' Considering he'd probably just landed another animal on the family at Folly Farm, he could hardly ask if they'd mind him getting a companion for Fred. It had taken quite some time for Rachel to accept him. He didn't want to push his luck.

*　*　*

Sam took over Duke's care. He'd listened carefully as Merlyn explained about the old dog's condition, and he'd instantly formed a bond with him. For his part, Duke seemed to like having the young boy around. He spent most of the day, when Sam was at school, fast asleep on his bed, but upon Sam's return he would wake up and wander into the living room to say hello. The two of them would sit together on the sofa, Duke's head on Sam's lap as they watched television together. Although Janie had control of the dog's medication, Sam always reminded her when it was time for Duke's next tablet, and praised Duke thoroughly for taking his pills *like a good boy*.

Xander was quite surprised, but relieved, that Rachel seemed happy to have Duke around, and she was looking much brighter in herself lately. He wasn't sure what the reason was, but he hoped it would last. She looked younger somehow. The tired, strained look had left her eyes, and she smiled far more often. It was good to see.

He'd decided to take her and Janie some flowers as a thank-you for giving a home to both Duke and Fred. He'd never imagined, when he chose to run away to Bramblewick, that he'd end up saving not one, but two animals from death, and he wouldn't have been able to do it without Janie's say-so and Rachel's agreement.

Maudie's shop didn't exactly have the greatest selection of flowers, but Xander managed to find two decent bunches, and added some chocolate and a comic for Sam — having been assured by Maudie that it was suitable for a seven-year-old boy, and very popular with the local children around his age.

'Mr South.'

Xander looked around in surprise as someone said his name in a rather anxious tone. It was a young woman, and he thought for a minute that she was going to ask him for his autograph or enquire if she could have her photograph taken with him. It wouldn't be the first time that a total stranger had pleaded that he smile at her phone as she took a selfie. He'd grown a bit tired of it, truthfully, but tried never to let that show. Being pleasant to a fan could make their day, and who knew what they were going through in real life? If he could bring a smile to someone's face, it was worth five minutes of his time. He smiled brightly at the woman. 'What can I do for you?'

To his surprise, she grabbed his arm and pulled him away from the counter. He glanced back anxiously at the flowers, chocolate and comic lying there, but Maudie merely nodded at him reassuringly. 'If you want a photo — '

'I came all the way from Oddborough to speak to you. Just walked through my mum's gate and saw you come in here. My mum lives in Bramblewick, you see, and she told me all about you and what you did for Duke. I thought you'd be the one to help.'

'Help? Help with what?'

'It's Little Red.' The woman's eyes filled with tears. 'I don't know what to do about him.'

'Little Red?' Xander frowned. 'I'm sorry. I don't — '

'My neighbour's kitten. Oh, Mr South, it's awful.'

Xander heard the distress in her voice and, after giving Maudie an apologetic look, steered the young woman outside. He led her to the bench on the green overlooking the beck, and gave her an encouraging smile. 'Why don't you start from the beginning? What's your name?'

'Sorry, I should have said. I'm Jacquie.' She took a tissue from her pocket and mopped her eyes. 'It's about Little Red. Well, all of them really, but Little Red's the main problem. My next-door neighbour has a cat. She's a lovely little thing, but they don't look after her. She's had two lots of kittens already and she's barely an adult herself. Anyway, this latest litter — ' She gulped and wiped her eyes again. 'Four of them, Mr South. And my neighbour wasn't happy about it, I can tell you, although she's always blooming cheerful when she sells them. Sold the last five for twenty-five pounds each, and that put a smile on her face. Anyway, she's got this little boy, you see. Proper little demon, he is. And, and — '

Xander found himself putting his hand on her shoulder, which was something he tended to avoid. You never knew what you might be accused of these days, and in his situation you couldn't be too careful. Something about this young woman made him throw caution to the wind. He had a feeling it wouldn't even occur to her to exploit him. She was genuinely upset, and he wanted to comfort her. 'What happened, Jacquie? What are you trying to tell me?'

'The little lad. He's got a proper temper on him. He threw Little Red against the wall.' She looked up at him, her eyes brimming with tears. 'Tiny little thing, he is, and the boy did that to him.'

'I suppose a two-year-old wouldn't understand,' he murmured, trying not to feel anger.

'You don't know him. Thought it was funny. But the point is, her, that woman, she did nothing about it. Left Little Red to suffer for three days. Admitted to me that she thought he'd just die, so left

142

him to it. He was only nine days old, Mr South! Have you ever heard anything so cruel?'

Xander felt sick. He shook his head, feeling helpless. 'And he didn't die, I take it?'

'When I went round there, and saw Little Red, I couldn't believe he'd survived. She told me all about it. Whining at me, she was, like he was an inconvenience. And I had to fish another kitten out of the toilet where the demon kid had just dropped him. He was trying to flush the chain.'

'Good grief! They need rescuing.'

'Oh, don't worry. Me and my Ian took them away, and the cat with them. Offered her a hundred pounds for them all and told her if she didn't hand them over we'd report her. She wasn't happy, but tough. They're all at ours, and they're staying there until the kittens can go to a good home. We'll keep Bonny — that's the cat. Get her spayed. No more kittens.' She took a deep breath. 'But Little Red . . . He's not good, Mr South. He can't walk, and he was crying all last night.'

'Have you taken him to a vet?'

'Of course we did. We took him to a local vet in Oddborough, first thing this morning. Not much cop, in my opinion. Budget vet — does treatments at cut price for families on low incomes. Don't judge us. It nearly broke us forking out a hundred quid for the kittens and Bonny. We couldn't afford much. My Ian's only just above minimum wage.'

'I wasn't judging you,' Xander assured her. 'I think you've been wonderful. What did the vet say?'

'That Little Red should be put down.' She lifted her chin defiantly. 'I wouldn't let him do it. Little one deserves a chance, don't you think? Walked out of the surgery with Little Red in my arms, and caught the first bus out here. I heard what you did for that horse, and for Duke. Whole village is talking about it. My mum says everyone's really impressed with you.'

Xander shuffled uncomfortably on

the bench. They were? He hadn't even been aware that the villagers knew about Fred and Duke. Then again, it was a small village. Word would spread, he supposed. 'Maybe we need a second opinion. Little Red should see another vet. There's a very good one in this village.'

Jacquie's face broke into a smile. 'I hoped you'd say that. Thing is, I can't afford it, so . . . '

'No problem. I'll ring Merlyn now, see if we can get Little Red in. How soon could you get him to Bramblewick?'

'He's here. I brought him with me. He's at my mum's right now.'

'You brought him on the bus?'

'I had no choice. I had no money left for a taxi. He was in a cat carrier, all padded out with blankets. He was secure, don't worry.' Her lip began to tremble. 'What else could I do?'

'Nothing, nothing. Don't worry.' He patted her hand, then withdrew hastily. 'I'll give Merlyn a call right now.'

'I'm so grateful to you,' Jacquie said,

leaning back on the bench and relaxing for the first time. 'Mum said you'd know what to do.'

As Xander put the phone to his ear and waited for the vet to answer his call, he couldn't help wondering exactly what he was getting himself into. His reputation was spreading — but it was Janie and Rachel at Folly Farm who had taken the animals in. A horse, an ancient dog, now a badly-damaged kitten. What on earth would they say to that? Always supposing Merlyn could save him, of course. In spite of it all, Xander found himself praying that Merlyn would disagree with the Oddborough vet. The thought of destroying a twelve-day-old kitten was simply unbearable.

9

Merlyn had squeezed Little Red into his surgery, but he wasn't very hopeful when he saw the state of him. 'You're making a habit of this,' he joked with Xander. 'We'll have to start calling you St Francis at this rate.'

Xander had paid for a taxi all the way back to Oddborough for Jacquie, after thanking her for bringing Little Red to him. She was openly crying when she left him, and had hardly been able to thank him enough. 'You're an angel, that's what you are. Thank you, Mr South. Thank you so much.'

'It's no trouble,' he'd assured her. 'Little Red will be fine, and I'll keep you informed on his progress.'

He'd given her a cheery smile as the taxi pulled away, but had then taken a deep breath and glanced down at the kitten in the cardboard box in his arms.

'Well, little fella. Time to take you to your new home. God willing.'

Anxiety had overwhelmed him as he approached Folly Farm, his stomach churning with nerves. He had a damn cheek, even he knew it. What would Janie and Rachel say this time? Janie might be okay, although even she'd probably think he was pushing it. But Rachel? Rachel had been like a different person around him recently, and she'd really taken to Duke; but she might think he was taking advantage of them, and then what would happen? Would she withdraw again? Become the mistrustful, wary woman she'd been until very recently? But what else, he asked himself, as he entered the farmyard, could he do? Mrs Lovelace wouldn't have a cat in the cottage, he knew that for sure. The only thing he could think of was finding another place to stay; but that would take time, and Little Red didn't have much time. He needed a home right now. Maybe if he could promise them it wouldn't be for long. Just until he found another rental home.

Janie's eyes widened when she opened the door and saw him standing there, holding the cardboard box, his expression clearly showing the mixture of guilt, embarrassment and hope that he was feeling. 'What on earth have you got for us now?' she said, but to his relief she gave him a broad smile and ushered him in.

The farmhouse seemed to wrap itself around him as he walked into the kitchen, giving him a warm hug. Xander felt the tension seep out of him, as he placed the box on the big, scrubbed pine table. He felt a pang of anxiety as the door opened and Rachel and Sam walked in. He'd assumed they'd be at work and school, then realised it was Saturday. He'd been on holiday so long, he'd quite lost track of the days.

'What is it?' Sam peered into the box and let out a cry of wonder at the sight of a tiny ginger kitten, fast asleep in his blanket.

'Another rescue case?' Rachel raised an eyebrow and Xander gave her a sheepish smile.

''Fraid so.'

Janie put the kettle on. 'Let's have a nice cup of tea, and you can tell us all about it,' she said.

Ten minutes later, Xander put down his cup and looked around at the others sitting at the table, listening agog to his every word. 'So, you see, I had no choice really. I had to take him to Merlyn, get another opinion.'

'And what did Merlyn say?' Janie's eyes, he noticed, were brimming with tears, but Rachel looked terrible. Her face was pale, and her eyes were large and full of pain. She looked completely stricken by Little Red's story, which surprised him.

'Poor little thing's too young to have any pain relief. The best thing we can do is restrict his movement, keep him warm, and feed him regularly. He gave me that cardboard box for him because it's just big enough for a blanket and a small litter tray.' He glanced around at them all apologetically. 'He's to be fed warm cat meat every three hours for the next three days, and then I've to take him back to the surgery. If he survives.'

Janie shook her head. 'Poor little mite. Well, it's no trouble. We'll make sure he's fed every three hours, so don't you worry about that.'

Xander felt weak with relief. 'You'll take him?'

'Of course we'll take him. Did you ever doubt it?' She gave him a knowing smile, but he couldn't smile back. Not yet. Not until he knew Rachel's reaction.

He glanced over at her. 'Rachel? Is that okay with you?'

He saw her swallow hard, then she nodded. 'Of course it's okay with me, Xander. We won't let Little Red die. He's going to be okay, I promise. We'll do everything we can for him.'

★ ★ ★

Rachel was glad to get home from work. The surgery was rather chaotic, because the builders had moved in to begin work on the extension. The waiting room was currently half its previous size, as the building was being reconfigured to allow for the work to be carried out. Patients were grumpy and complaining; the noise was already proving distracting; and to top it all, Holly had gone home unwell, leaving Anna to deal with all the admin alone — though, really, there was no choice. Holly was clearly suffering. 'My own fault,' she'd moaned as she returned from the toilets yet again. 'I ate a dodgy pasty. Well past its sell-by date, but I couldn't resist. I'm ever so sorry, Anna.' It had been a stressful afternoon all round, and Rachel was looking forward to a long, hot shower and a night in front of the television.

She tried to deny the fluttering in her stomach as she entered the hallway of the farmhouse and heard Xander's voice coming from the living room. He was here again? *He might as well just move in, he's here so often these days,* Rachel thought grumpily. He'd be there to see how Little Red had got on, though, and she could hardly blame him for that. She was quite eager to know how he'd got on herself. Her mum had taken the kitten to the vet that afternoon, and they were all quite anxious about the verdict.

'You're home!' Her mother smiled up at her as she walked into the living room. Sam beamed at her, too, which was always comforting. He'd been smiling a lot more recently, she reflected. He was sitting on the sofa, Duke lying across his knee, one hand stroking the dog's silky head. He had dog hair on his school jumper, she noticed ruefully. He should have got changed as soon as he came home from school. Beside him, Xander sat nursing the tiny kitten on a blanket on his lap. Rachel's heart melted at the contented expression on Little Red's face, as Xander gently stroked him between his ears.

'Did you have a good day at work, Rachel?' Her mother pulled herself up from the armchair. 'I'll put the kettle on.'

'Sit down, Mum. I'll make us all a drink in a minute,' Rachel told her firmly. 'Firstly, what happened with Little Red?'

She felt, rather than saw, Xander's smile of warm approval, and tried not to be swayed by it. She was only interested in the kitten, she reminded herself, and fixed her gaze on her mum.

'He may need surgery.' Her mother sighed, glancing over at the pretty but beleaguered kitten.

'Aw, the poor little mite.' Rachel shook her head. It was such a shame, although she'd suspected it might happen. Little Red had shown signs of improvement over the last few days, developing an appetite for the cat food. But his skin had started to peel, and sores had developed on his back feet. Merlyn had initially thought they were burns. A week or so later, the toes on his back foot had begun to turn black, and his claws had fallen off.

'The toes are dead. They'll probably need removing,' her mother continued. 'But the good news is, he seems to be improving in himself. Merlyn was quite pleased with him in other respects. And he was rather impressed by the way the little thing managed to drag himself along the table in the consulting room.'

'He's a fighter all right,' Xander said, smiling proudly down at the kitten. 'What do you say, Sam? Tough little guy, right? A survivor.'

Sam nodded and carefully fondled Little Red's ears. 'He's strong for a baby, isn't he?'

'He is that,' Janie said fondly. 'Maybe we ought to give him a proper name, now that it looks as if he's going to make it. Little Red won't be much use to him when he's a full-grown cat. It will be embarrassing for him.'

'Maybe Sam could think of a new name for him,' Xander suggested. Rachel shot him a look of gratitude.

Sam looked thrilled. 'Really? Can I?'

'I don't see why not. Have you got any ideas?'

Sam considered for a moment. 'Xander just said he's a survivor,' he said thoughtfully. 'And he's right. We're doing all about that at school at the moment. How only the strongest survive. Evolution.'

'Ah yes, evolution.' Xander smiled at him. 'I can see where this is going.'

'So, can we call him Darwin? Maybe it might bring him luck. Mr Darwin said that nature makes sure the strongest live, and our kitten must be ever so strong, because look what he's been through, but he's still here, and he's teaching himself to get around, even though he can't walk properly. What do you think?'

'I think it's a perfect name,' Rachel said, walking over to stroke the kitten. 'Welcome to Folly Farm, Darwin. I hope you'll be very happy in your new home.'

'I'll tell you what else Merlyn said,'

her mum said suddenly. 'About Fred.' She gave Xander a knowing look. 'Reckons he needs some company. Horses shouldn't be kept on their own. Now, what shall we do about that?'

Sam's face lit up. 'We could get a cow,' he said. 'Then we could have our own milk and make our own butter.' He pulled a face. 'It takes ages, though. We did it at my old school. We put milk in a big jar, and we all had to take turns shaking it, and we were doing it for hours and hours. It turned to butter in the end, though, but we weren't allowed to eat it. Mrs Dale said — ' He screwed up his nose and thought for a moment. ' — health and safety rules. That was it.'

'Hmm. Well, I think a cow's being a bit ambitious,' Rachel said firmly. She ruffled his hair, then straightened. 'I'll put the kettle on, shall I?'

'I'll help you. Sam, can I put you on kitten duty?' Xander carefully passed him the blanket in which Darwin nestled, then rose and followed Rachel to the kitchen.

'I can manage four drinks on my own,' she told him, laughing rather awkwardly as he filled the kettle with water.

'I know. I just — ' Xander flicked the switch and turned to look at her, seeming uncomfortable suddenly. 'I just wanted to say thank you. I know I've landed three animals on you now, and you could have said no to any one, or all of them, but you haven't. I really can't tell you how grateful I am.'

'Don't be daft.' She shrugged, reaching into the cupboard for mugs. 'Fred's no bother, out in the field, and mum would never have abandoned Duke. She remembers him as a pup and couldn't have had him put to sleep.'

'But Little — I mean, Darwin. There was no reason for you to take him in. It was just so kind of you all. You're an extraordinary family.'

'We're really not.' Rachel's voice shook.

'Yes, you are. Seriously, Rachel. You've been amazing. I'm so — '

'Xander, please don't.'

She couldn't keep the distress from

her voice, and he stopped, a puzzled look on his face. 'What is it?'

She bit her lip, wondering if she could bear to tell him the awful truth. Which was worse? Hearing him praise her for her kindness, when she really didn't deserve it, or seeing the look on his face when she told him the sort of woman she actually was?

He'd moved closer without her realising it, and his hands were on her shoulders, his eyes gazing into hers. 'Please don't do this again. I didn't mean to upset you.'

'You didn't.' She shook her head, half hoping he would move away and half hoping he wouldn't. 'You don't understand, really you don't.'

'Then why don't you tell me,' he said gently.

His blue eyes were warm with sympathy, and she thought she could quite easily tell him everything. How tempting to finally unburden herself to someone, to pour out all the guilt and fear and pain. But then the look in those blue eyes would change. She'd be *that woman* again, the way she had been at her old job, with her old neighbours. *Poor Rachel.* Poor downtrodden, deluded, stupid Rachel. The woman who asked for everything she got. The woman who put her own fears ahead of her child's needs. *That Rachel* whom she so despised.

'It doesn't matter,' she said, her voice heavy with regret.

He didn't let go. Instead, one hand gently stroked her cheek. 'I think it does, and I'd like to help.'

She took a deep breath. Maybe there was one thing she could confess — something she could get off her chest. She could only hope he would understand, although she wasn't sure how when she couldn't understand it herself. 'It's sort of a — a penance,' she admitted, turning away from him and picking up the tea canister with shaking hands.

He sounded baffled. 'A penance? For what?'

'Years ago, Grant — my husband

— he did something awful, and I knew about it and stayed with him anyway.'

'What did he do?' A kind, caring voice. How could someone with that voice ever understand?

'He drowned three kittens.' She heard the catch in her voice and busied herself making tea, trying to harden her heart as best she could. The memory always made her feel sick to her stomach. She could still hear the pitiful cries coming from that sack. 'His mother's cat had given birth, and his mother didn't want them. She asked him to get rid of them, and that was his solution. I — I saw him do it. I tried to stop him, really I did, but he just — he took no notice.' It was the first bruise she'd ever got from him, she remembered. She'd hardly noticed the pain, swamped with grief over the fate of those poor little creatures drowning before her eyes. She'd known then, really, what Grant was. She should have left him, walked away. How could she love a man who would do something so despicable? *But Sam had been a tiny baby*, her inner voice protested. She'd been scared, and vulnerable. No excuses, though. She should have got away from Grant before he could start to inflict his view of the world upon their son. She'd been a coward.

Slowly, she turned to Xander, dreading the look of contempt in his eyes. Instead, she saw him watching her with something that looked surprisingly like compassion.

'That must have been horrible for you,' he said softly. 'I'm so sorry, Rachel.'

Tears welled up in her eyes. 'It was. But not as horrible as it was for those poor little kittens! So you see, that's why I wanted to help Darwin. Put it right somehow. I know it won't bring those other kittens back, but I thought, if I could just help him, somehow it would start to — to — '

'Ease the pain.' He put his arms around her and held her carefully. 'I understand that.'

He did? She closed her eyes,

breathing in the smell of his hair, skin, and aftershave, and realising that, for the first time in what seemed like forever, the scent of a man didn't fill her with revulsion and fear. She could stay in his arms forever, feeling safe, secure.

Hastily, she pulled away. 'Tea,' she said briskly. 'Can you carry yours and Mum's? I'll take mine and Sam's.'

The conversation was over. The moment had passed, and the tone had changed. How could it be any different? Rachel gave Xander a bright smile. 'Then I'll open the biscuits.'

10

Leaning back in his chair, Xander ran a hand across his tired eyes and sighed. Another email from Penny.

'You need to make a decision, and I'm talking option A or option B! Don't even think about option C, because that's *not* an option — it's professional suicide. Time's running out. Decide soon, because if you don't, they'll make a decision for you. Get a grip, Xander!'

Poor Penny. She simply couldn't understand his dilemma. As she saw it, he had two choices, and they were good choices. She'd dismissed his third option out of hand, yet that was the one that most appealed to him.

'Time for all that when your looks go, and they only want you for character parts. Right now, you're eye candy. Make the most of it, sunshine, because nothing lasts forever.'

He looked over at Belle and Rumpel who were lying on their bed, watching him hopefully. Time for a walk. A bit of fresh April air would blow the cobwebs away and help him think. Maybe.

The grass verges in the village were still bright with daffodils. They'd flowered late this year, because of the bitterly cold weather throughout February and March. They lined the banks of the beck too, making a cheerful picture as Xander crossed the little stone bridge and headed out along the footpath across the fields, the dogs pulling eagerly at their leads. It was a cool day, but the sky was blue and clear, and the sun was brightening the landscape, even if it wasn't warming it up that much.

The footpath was well-used by the villagers, skirting the farmers' fields and cutting around woodland, heading across the moors to Hatton-le-Dale, the next village. Xander wasn't surprised to see someone else walking their dog, although he was a little taken aback when the woman stopped him, her voice brisk, her face quite serious.

'Mr South?'

He wasn't entirely sure if he was Mr North or Mr South at the moment, so he just nodded, smiled, and said hello, praying whoever it was wouldn't keep him talking about *Lord Curtis Investigates* for long.

'I was really hoping to see you today. I considered visiting you at Sweet Briar, but I knew you walked the dawgs along here every day, so . . . '

She did? Wow, he'd really have to change his routine. Any weird stalker could follow him and — well, it didn't bear thinking about.

'How can I help you? If it's an autograph — ' Although, truthfully, she didn't look like a fan. She looked like a middle-aged version of the Queen, with her headscarf and green wellies and assured manner.

'What? Oh no, nothing like that.' The woman sounded quite dismissive, and he wasn't sure whether to be relieved or insulted. 'No, it's Mabel and Maureen.'

'Mabel and Maureen who?' Xander frowned. 'I'm sorry. I'm not sure I'm following.'

The woman's springer spaniel was straining at the lead. She eyed the poodles warily. 'Are your dawgs all right with other dawgs?'

'Absolutely fine,' he assured her, wondering what she was talking about now.

The woman bent down, unclipped her spaniel's lead, and watched as he investigated Belle and Rumpel with great interest. There was a general wagging of tails and a lot of sniffing, then the spaniel shot off into the woods.

'Will he be all right in there?'

'What?' The woman shook her head impatiently. 'Oh, yes, yes, he's fine. He goes there every day. Rabbits. Now, Mr South, about Mabel and Maureen.'

'Who are these people?'

'Not people at all. Goats. My aunt's goats.'

Xander wondered if the woman was

quite right in the head. What did a stranger's goats have to do with him? 'Your aunt's goats?'

She stared at him as if he were stupid. 'Yes. Goats,' she said, emphasising the words as though he had hearing difficulties too. 'Now,' she said, holding up a hand as he opened his mouth to speak, 'I'm well aware that goats aren't everyone's favourite animals. Lord knows, I can't stand the nasty, greedy creatures, but my aunt loved them. What could we do? Now, of course, we're stuck, because who on earth wants to take in goats?'

Xander's heart sank. He had a horrible feeling he knew where this conversation was heading.

'She's dead, you see.'

'Who? Mabel or Maureen?'

The woman tutted. 'My aunt. Do try to pay attention, Mr South. Now, I know you have a fondness for animals. It's common knowledge what's going on up at the farm, and since we've exhausted all other possibilities we

168

thought of you.'

'Er, thanks. I think.' Xander frowned. So, she wanted him to take the goats that belonged to her aunt who had now died? 'You're asking me to take on Mabel and Maureen?'

'Don't worry, I don't expect you to pay me for them,' she said, with breathtaking cheek. 'They're elderly. No use to anyone, really, but my aunt made me promise I'd find a good home for them, and I'm a woman of my word, even if I do think my aunt was barking mad and goats are vile. So, shall I get Rex to drop them orf at the farm this evening?'

'Rex?' Xander felt bewildered. This woman took no prisoners, that was for sure.

'My husband. He'll put them in the trailer, and they should be with you around six. Wonderful. So glad we got that sorted out. Such a relief.' She gave him a brittle smile, wrapped the lead around her hand, and strode off before Xander could even collect his thoughts, never mind start to protest.

Belle and Rumpel peered up at him, looking as stunned as he felt.

Xander gave a big sigh. 'Change of plan, guys. Looks like we'd better take a walk to the farm. I have some news to break to Janie. Oh boy, she's going to love me.'

★   ★   ★

As it turned out, Janie was in a radiant mood, and didn't seem in the slightest put out when Xander dropped the news on her that Folly Farm was about to be invaded by elderly goats.

'How marvellous. I love goats. And they'll be company for Fred, after all. That's that sorted. Would you like to try one of my scones, Xander?'

Xander shook his head in wonder. 'You take everything on the chin, don't you? Does nothing faze you, Janie?'

She gave him a sad smile. 'When you've seen your livelihood destroyed, your husband broken, lost the love of

170

your life, and worried yourself sick about your only child and grandson, having a couple of goats landed on you is the least of your worries.' She beckoned him in. 'Besides,' she added brightly, 'I'm in a very good mood today. Thinking about Duke's owner, Cassie, reminded me of the reading group we used to have in the village, so I've been making a few calls today; and the upshot is, we're reviving it. Only a handful of us, but it's a start, and it will be wonderful to get out and about again. I seem to have been hiding away up here for ages. Time to begin socialising again. Merlyn's going, too. It will be good for him to develop a hobby. It's all work and no play with him.'

'That's wonderful.' He smiled, genuinely delighted for her.

'Elaine was a bit doubtful about having a man in the group — especially a vet. She suspects he'll want us to read non-stop James Herriot, but I'm sure he'll be less annoying than she is. Last time we ran it, she was always demanding we read the most sickeningly gory thrillers. Still, I'm sure we can make some sort of deal. Have a scone,' she said, handing him a plate bearing a plain scone, a blob of jam, and a dollop of clotted cream. 'Cup of tea to go with it?' she added, filling the kettle. How could he refuse such a delicious and unexpected treat?

'How's Darwin doing?' he enquired. 'And where's Duke?' he added, noting that the dog wasn't lying in his usual place beside the sofa in the kitchen.

'Duke's on Sam's bed,' Janie said, turning to face him as she waited for the tea to mash. 'That dog's become so attached to Sam that he doesn't seem to want to be parted from him. We thought it would be less stressful if they stayed together; and Sam, of course, was delighted.'

'And Rachel agreed to that?' Xander was amazed. He couldn't imagine her being thrilled that a dog was lying on her son's bed every night.

Even Janie looked a bit bewildered. 'You know what? She actually did. And she didn't take much persuading. Sam just said he didn't want Duke to feel lonely or left out at night, and she gave in, just like that. Very unexpected, I must say. Duke gets very tired very quickly, and spends most of the day up there asleep, to be honest. He comes downstairs when Sam gets home from school, but he knows when it's bedtime again. He starts looking hopefully at the door, then at Sam. He's quite a useful reminder for Rachel that it's that time again, actually.' She laughed.

'And Darwin?'

'Oh, bless him. He's managing to get around. Caught him half in Duke's water bowl yesterday, copying Duke as he drank the water. Mind you, he's a funny little thing. Doesn't lap water at all — he sucks it up. Never seen anything like it. He's asleep in the living room at the moment. He'll spend the evening on Rachel's lap, no doubt. She's devoted to him.'

Xander smiled, glad that Darwin was helping Rachel lay her ghosts to rest. He realised suddenly that he quite envied Darwin, being the centre of her attention all evening, being so close to her . . .

Pushing the thought aside, he reached eagerly for the mug of tea Janie offered him and concentrated on the task of devouring his scone. Ten minutes later, he pushed his plate away rather regretfully, and informed Janie that she made the best ones he'd ever tasted. 'And I've eaten scones in some of the finest places,' he assured her. 'That was in a class of its own.'

'Thank you very much,' she said, laughing. 'I think I can see why you got the part of a charmer like Lord Curtis.'

At the mention of his name, Xander's mood darkened and he sighed.

Janie leaned forward, her expression curious. 'How much longer will you be here for? Do you start filming again soon?'

He shook his head. 'If a new series goes ahead, they'll probably want me back filming in September. But it's a big if. I haven't signed the contract yet, and they're getting quite antsy about the whole thing.'

'Oh?' She broke off a piece of scone and fed it to the poodles. 'Is there a reason you're delaying?'

'Truthfully? I'm really not sure if I want to be Lord Bay Curtis any more. We've done six series of this now and, personally, I think it's had its day. Besides, there are other things I'd like to do.'

'Like what?'

'I've had quite a few offers, but two in particular are giving me sleepless nights. My agent, Penny, wants me to ditch the show and sign up for a feature film. It's a big deal. Hollywood, lead role. It would make me a fortune.'

'Sounds wonderful,' she said, eyeing him closely. 'You don't seem too thrilled, though.'

He shrugged. 'It's Action Man stuff,' he said dismissively. 'I really don't think it's something I'm going to love doing, put it that way. Besides — Hollywood.' He tutted. 'It's not all it's cracked up to be. I've worked there a lot, and I've seen things that would make your hair curl. It's not real. It's not home. It's a factory, churning out stuff that — mostly — I don't want to be involved with.' He looked thoughtful. 'You know, a few years ago I'd have bitten their hand off for that sort of opportunity. Funny how you start to see things differently.'

'So, what's the other one?' Seeing his puzzled expression, she said gently, 'You said you had two particular offers. What's the other one?'

'Oh.' He leaned back in his chair and folded his arms. 'Something that Penny won't even contemplate. Theatre. It's a new play by an up-and-coming writer, and I really loved the script. I mean, I *really* loved it. The money's dismal, but I've got more money now than I know what to do with, and I think it could be a valuable and interesting experience.' He allowed himself to imagine it for a moment. The audience, the theatre, the excitement of performing in front of real people in real time, instant feedback, the adrenaline rush . . . 'It's been years since I did theatre. I've missed it.'

'Surely it's up to you?' Janie said. 'Your decision what you do with your career.'

'It's not that simple.' Xander frowned, thinking of Penny. 'My agent — she's stuck by me through all the bad times. When no one else wanted to know, she was there for me. I owe her.'

'That's very kind of you, Xander.'

'Not at all. It's a fact. She believed in me. She's a good friend.'

'But surely a friend would want you to be happy in what you're doing?'

His finger circled the rim of his teacup. 'She does. Fact is, Penny and I are a team. When I landed the Curtis role, and my name got out there, I could have left her to go with a bigger agent. Penny knows that. She always says she owes me, too. I brought new clients to her — some have made it big. The truth is, our relationship is much deeper than agent and client. We both want the best for each other.'

'I see.' Janie sounded a little regretful, which puzzled him. 'I take it you and Penny are — what do they say these days — an item?'

Xander laughed. 'Me and Penny? Never! She's sixty-two, for one thing. Don't get me wrong, she's a beautiful lady and I love her to bits, but she's happily married; and the only man who gets a look-in, apart from her husband, is her grandson Josh, who's just had his third birthday. No, if anything, Penny mothers me. That's why I don't want to let her down.'

Janie looked thoughtful. 'If you were my son, I'd want you to follow your heart and your passion. Nothing matters more.'

'Penny's seen me destitute. She's covered my rent more than once. I think she's scared I'll throw it all away, and that this *theatre obsession*, as she labels it, would be the start of a slippery slope.'

Janie raised an eyebrow. 'Are you sure there's not just a little part of you that's scared, too? Maybe you're using Penny as an excuse.'

He was quiet for a moment, studying his empty cup through narrowed eyes. 'You know,' he said slowly, 'you may be on to something there.'

'It's not surprising you're anxious, Xander,' she assured him. 'You clearly had to endure terrible poverty and hardship while waiting for your big break. Lord Curtis saved you, made you a star, made you a fortune. To give up on him now must be terribly scary after — how long is it? Six years?'

Xander nodded. 'A lot's happened in those six years. When I started on that show, I had nothing. Wild horses wouldn't have made me ask my parents for a handout, and I can't tell you how many times I had nothing in the cupboards but a box of porridge oats or a few potatoes. It made me. I owe it such a lot. But I strongly believe that it's run its course. I know the fans want more, and the producers are saying we should give it one final series before bowing out, but I just don't know. Yet, I don't want to let everyone down — so many people are involved in *Lord Curtis Investigates*, and they're relying on me to continue for the sake of their jobs.'

'But Penny would prefer you to do the film in America?'

'The Americans love Lord Curtis. I spent weeks out there last spring, promoting the show, having meetings and lunches with the big guns over there. That's how I got offered the role in this film. It's incredibly flattering. I understand Penny's enthusiasm. Crack America and you've really made it. If I turn this job down, will they ever ask me again?'

'Do you want them to ask you again?'

'What sort of question is that?'

'A serious one. Is a Hollywood film high on your wish list? Or is it just something you think you ought to want, but in reality you'd hate it? How much fame do you need?'

Xander rubbed his chin. 'You ask all the right questions, don't you?'

'I just think it's time you did the same. It sounds to me like money isn't an issue for you.'

'It's not,' he admitted. 'Truthfully, if I never worked again, I've made more than enough to keep me in comfort for the rest of my life.'

'Then it's a question of following your heart's desire. Forget all this worrying about what Penny says. She's an agent, and she's doing what she thinks is best for you, but she'll want you to be happy in what you're doing, I'm sure. Besides, you said yourself, she has other big clients now. Let her focus on their careers. I think you're too hard on yourself. The village is agog that you're staying here. So many people seem to know who you are, and love your work. If you turn down one film, it's not going to finish you off. There'll be other roles. Anyway, what's wrong with doing a play? It might not earn you big money, but theatre work seems to give actors huge credibility. The play's the thing, dah-ling.'

Xander couldn't help but laugh. 'You're too clever for your own good. Thanks, Janie. I'll have a good think about it and then get in touch with Penny. I'm running out of time on all counts, to be honest. If I don't make the decision soon, no one will want me.'

'That will never happen,' she assured him. 'Now, are you going to be here at six when these goats arrive? Only, from what you said about this pushy woman, I don't really fancy dealing with her husband alone. If he's anything like her, he'll probably end up charging me for taking them!'

'Will Rachel be home?'

'Not at six. She's working until that time tonight. Goodness knows what she'll make of two new arrivals to the farm. We're turning into Noah's Ark here.'

'I really do appreciate it,' Xander told her warmly. 'And, of course, you won't be out of pocket.'

'Oh, get away with you,' she said. 'I'll see you at six. Don't be late!'

'I won't. I think the least I can do is deal with the chap, and also explain to Rachel what happened when she turns up.'

'I'm sure she won't mind. We all agreed with Merlyn that Fred needs company. The goats will be perfect. Problem solved.'

One problem, at least, thought Xander. Now he just had to figure out what to do with the tiny little problem of his career.

11

Rachel eyed Anna worriedly. 'You look dreadful. Sit down for a moment before you fall down.'

Anna evidently needed no persuading. 'Thanks, Rachel. I think I'll have to.' She almost collapsed onto the chair and took some deep breaths. 'I feel so nauseated.'

'Sounds like it's your turn to have Holly's bug,' Rachel said. 'Oh crikey, I hope this doesn't get passed around all of us. Can you imagine if we all got it?'

'Don't even joke about it,' Anna said.

Holly looked suitably guilty. 'Sorry, Anna. I was sure it was down to eating that out-of-date pasty, too. Obviously, it was something more than that. Really feel bad that I've passed it to you.'

Anna gulped. Clearly the mention of pasties hadn't helped. Rachel saw the beads of sweat on her forehead, the look of panic in her eyes. Instinctively, she grabbed the waste bin and practically thrust it under Anna's head, just in time. Trying not to feel nauseated herself, Rachel held the bin in place with one hand, pulling her colleague's hair away from her face with the other, as the illness got the better of poor Anna.

Holly looked green and opened the window, just as Connor appeared in the office. 'Have we got any — Anna, what's wrong?'

'Think she's caught my bug, Doc,' Holly said sheepishly. 'Sorry and all that.'

Connor crouched down in front of his wife, who was now leaning back in her chair looking positively grey. He handed her some tissues, and she dabbed at her mouth with a rather shaky hand. 'No work for you today,' he told her firmly. 'Go on, get your coat and go home for a lie-down. We'll manage.'

'But there's a pile of prescriptions to be printed.'

'I can do those,' Holly assured her. 'If

there's anything too complicated, I'm sure one day won't make a difference, and the basic stuff I can do on my own. If there's anything urgent, I'll ask Connor or Riley to help.'

'Please, sweetheart, get yourself to bed for a couple of hours. I'll nip home at lunchtime and check on you, okay?' Connor's voice was pleading, and Anna gave in. She obviously felt too ill to put up much of a fight. Rachel sincerely hoped that whatever bug was attacking the surgery, it would stop with Anna. The last thing she needed was to pass something like that on to her mum or Sam. Or Xander.

Realising she'd included Xander in her family, she felt a lurch of anxiety in her stomach. 'Go on, off you go,' she said briskly. 'I'd better deal with this,' she added, wrinkling her nose as she glanced down at the waste bin. 'Good job there's a strong bin liner in there.'

'I'm ever so sorry, Rachel. Thanks so much for being there.'

'Oh, I've seen much worse,' Rachel

assured her, quite truthfully. As a nurse, she'd seen pretty much everything, and she'd developed a strong stomach; although she had to admit, she still found some things pretty nauseating.

Ten minutes later, Holly was working on the prescriptions, Anna had gone home, and Rachel was back in her consulting room, welcoming in her next patient.

A rather nervous-looking girl, with long, sandy-coloured hair and freckles, wandered in, taking her seat by Rachel's desk.

'Francesca Green, isn't it?' Rachel smiled reassuringly as the girl nodded. She was eighteen and had Type One diabetes. She was booked in to have bloods taken before her diabetes review in a fortnight's time. 'Don't look so nervous. It won't take long. Now, can you take off your jacket, please?'

Ten minutes later, Francesca was putting on her jacket once more, as Rachel labelled the tubes of blood ready to send off to the lab. When the girl didn't leave, Rachel glanced up, surprised to see her hovering by the desk, looking uncertain.

'Was there something you wanted to discuss, Francesca?' Rachel glanced at the time on her computer screen, hoping the girl wasn't about to launch into some plea for contraception advice or worse. She had a full clinic that morning, and didn't want to hurry the poor girl along, but she would really have to get her to make another appointment.

'It's about my pony.'

Well, Rachel certainly hadn't been expecting that. She stopped writing and gazed up at the young woman, puzzled. 'I'm sorry?'

Francesca seemed to decide it was now or never. She plonked herself down on the chair and stared at Rachel with wide, pleading eyes. 'She's over twenty now, and I can't ride her because she's far too small for me, but there was a young girl, Harriet, who used to ride her three or four days a week, so Dad never seemed to mind when I said I wouldn't part with her. But now Harriet's moved away from Bramblewick and I'm probably going away to university this summer, and no one else in my family knows or cares about ponies, and there's no one to look after her. Dad says she costs too much anyway, and she's just eating her head off for no reason, and it's time we thought about selling her on. But who's going to want her? She's old. And what if someone does buy her, but then doesn't look after her? How will I know? I'll be away, and anything could happen to her.'

'O-kay,' Rachel said slowly, not sure she was following.

'So, I thought, well, I needed to ask you — will you take her, please?'

'Me?' Rachel dropped her pen. 'I don't know much about ponies. I mean, I used to have one when I was a child, but I was completely useless at riding.'

'But it's what you do, isn't it, up at Folly Farm? Take in animals that no one else wants.'

Rachel gaped at her. 'Is it?'

'Everyone knows it is. You and your mum and that actor. You've opened a sort of sanctuary, haven't you?'

Rachel swallowed. Was that what everyone thought? Good grief. How had that happened? She thought of Fred and Duke and Darwin, and gave an inward sigh. It was pretty obvious how it had happened, really. It didn't take long for gossip to spread through a small village like Bramblewick, and they'd all clearly put two and two together and made five.

'We're not a sanctuary,' she said gently. 'It's really not like that. There were just a few unfortunate animals that we found out about and wanted to help.'

'But you already have one horse. And you've got loads of land. Would one little pony make that much difference? Please, Nurse. I don't want her to go to some awful strangers who might neglect her or mistreat her. Please. I'm seriously thinking of not going to uni, because I daren't leave her.'

'You can't throw your chance away like that,' Rachel told her, appalled. 'I'm sure if you speak to your parents, let them know how much this is upsetting you, they'll change their minds.'

'They already know.' She swallowed. 'Truth is, they can't afford her any more. Dad's had his hours cut at work. Times are a bit tough right now, and I do understand that, and I really do feel for them. I've been working part-time in Whitby to help towards her keep, but when I go away — if I go away — I won't be able to help any more. How can I expect Dad to fork out for her?' Her eyes filled with tears. 'If you won't have her, I don't know what else to do.'

Rachel closed her eyes. Talk about emotional blackmail. Another animal to care for, and she could hardly ask Xander for help, since this one would be nothing to do with him. Then she thought about Fred, all alone in the paddock behind the house, and sighed.

'Okay, Francesca. If it's okay with your parents, we'll take your pony. But we can't afford to buy her off you, you understand that?'

'I don't think Dad will mind that, as long as she gets a good home and I don't put up a fight about it.' Francesca's face was lit up with enthusiasm. 'Thank you so much, Nurse. I'll bring her round at the weekend, if that's okay?'

'You said someone used to ride her,' Rachel said thoughtfully. 'Is she still okay to be ridden? She's not too old?'

'Oh, no. I mean, she's not going to win any gymkhanas, but the vet told us that we should give her gentle exercise at least three or four times a week — you know, just a quiet hack out. It's good for her. Otherwise her joints might stiffen, and she could get depressed. She loves being ridden out, and she's ever so good. Really gentle. Never bucks or shies or anything. Bombproof.'

'Hmm.' Rachel thought about Sam. Maybe he'd like to learn to ride. An old, good-natured pony might be perfect for him. She was sure he'd love it more than she ever had. 'Okay, Francesca. If your parents agree, you can bring her round on Saturday with all her stuff, and we'll go over everything we need to know then.'

'Oh, thank you so much. I'll get Dad to ring you tonight. Honestly, he'll be fine about it.'

Rachel smiled as the young woman headed to the door, her whole demeanour changed. 'Oh, by the way, what's your pony's name?' she said, suddenly realising she hadn't asked.

Francesca smiled. 'Ginger — on account of her chestnut coat.'

Rachel rolled her eyes. Ginger! Well, of course she was called Ginger. It seemed Fred would have the perfect companion after all.

★   ★   ★

Rachel had worked through her lunch break, helping Holly catch up with admin. She'd rung her mum to warn her she wouldn't be home, and to tell her not to make her anything to eat.

193

'That's fine, Rachel. Poor Anna, I hope she'll be okay. Sounds like a nasty bug going around.'

'You're not wrong there, Mum. Let's hope it avoids me. I'll see you around half-past six.'

'Okay. I, er — I may have a surprise for you when you get home.'

Rachel hadn't liked the sound of that. Her mother's voice sounded distinctly guilty. 'Oh? What sort of surprise?'

'Dratted photocopier.' Holly slammed the paper drawer shut and glared at the machine. 'Why does it never work properly for me?'

Rachel rolled her eyes and gripped the phone tighter as her mother said, 'Oh, you'll see. Nothing to worry about, honestly.'

'Hmm.' It had been on the tip of her tongue to tell her mother that she'd solved Fred's loneliness problem, but maybe that was too big a conversation to have over the phone. Better to break it to her in person. There was no rush. After all, there would be no new arrivals at the farm until the weekend. 'If you say so. As long as you haven't landed us with a cow or six pigs or something.' She laughed at the very thought of it. Not that it would be funny if that really happened. Crikey, what would they do with six pigs? Perish the thought.

'Oh, not pigs, no.'

Rachel frowned. What did her mother mean by that?

'Rachel, help!'

Holly's shriek reached even Mrs Frost's ears. 'What's wrong? What's happening?'

'Rachel! It won't stop copying! I only wanted one! Do something!'

'Don't worry, Mum. It's only Holly having a fight with the photocopier again. Look, I'll see you tonight.' Rachel ended the call and rushed to help Holly, who was grabbing sheets of paper that the photocopier was hurling in her direction.

'Why won't it stop? I only wanted one copy. What's the stupid thing doing?'

Rachel peered at the screen and laughed. 'You've put the passcode in, instead of the number of copies you want. You're printing off thousands!'

'Oh, flipping heck! What do I do?'

Rachel pressed the cancel button, opened the paper drawer and said, 'There you go. Problem solved.'

Holly slumped. 'Phew! Thanks, Rachel. I'm really not cut out for this technology stuff.'

'You're in your twenties! This is supposed to be child's play for you.' Rachel grinned at her. 'You're just easily distracted, that's your trouble.'

Once she and Holly had tidied up the area around the photocopier, then settled down to get on with their respective tasks before lunch, Rachel had totally forgotten about her mother's comments. As she made her way home that evening, she thought about how she was going to break it to her that she'd agreed to take on yet another animal guest. And not exactly a small guest, either. It wasn't a rabbit or a guinea pig, but a pony, of all things. But it would be wonderful if Sam bonded with Ginger, she thought. He'd become quite attached to Fred, and actually being able to ride the pony might be the making of him. He'd bonded so beautifully with Duke and Darwin, much to her relief. Rachel was actually beginning to relax a little — to believe that maybe she hadn't left it too late, after all.

As she turned into the lane that led to Folly Farm, she had to pull over sharply as a large Range Rover, dragging a trailer, bounced along the track towards her. As it passed, the man sitting in the driving seat raised a gloved hand at her and nodded.

Rachel frowned. This lane led only to the farm. Who was this visitor — and, more to the point, what had been in that trailer?

Feeling increasingly worried, she continued her journey, pulling into the farmyard and trying to ignore the way her stomach leapt when she saw Xander standing beside her mother and

Sam just outside the barn.

Sam's face was bright with excitement as she climbed out of the car and walked slowly towards the little gathering. 'Mum, come and meet Mabel and Maureen!'

'What? Who on earth — ?'

Xander looked apologetic. 'My fault, I'm afraid.'

'I rather thought it would be,' Rachel said. 'What have you done now?'

Xander gave her a sheepish smile. 'I sort of got accosted by some woman on the footpath this morning. She needed a home for her aunt's goats, and I — '

'Goats?' She groaned. 'You're kidding!'

'Oh, but Rachel, they're adorable.' Her mother looked quite excited. 'They're quite elderly, and both female, obviously, so we don't have to worry about milking them. It's going to be fun. Goats are such mischievous, inquisitive creatures. I always wanted goats, but your father wouldn't hear of it. I can't imagine why. We've just got them nicely bedded down in the barn, and they're already eating their heads off as if they've been here forever.'

'They're ever so cute, Mum,' Sam assured her.

'And the good thing is,' Xander said, 'they can go out in the paddock with Fred, can't they? So, he'll have some company at last.'

Rachel shook her head. 'Not such a good idea. Firstly, Fred's probably never seen a goat in his life before. Goats are highly inquisitive and, to put it bluntly, they can be a real pain in the backside. If they annoyed Fred and he kicked out, they'd have no chance. It's best to keep them separate, but where they can see each other, so they get used to one another before even attempting to put them together.'

'Oh.' Her mother looked deflated. 'Well, maybe we can put them in the orchard? Fred will be able to see them, and — '

Rachel tried not to sound annoyed. 'They'd demolish the orchard! And they'd get out of there with no trouble. They're renowned escapologists.' She ran a weary hand through her hair. 'Do you know what hard work goats are? It's not a case of just sticking them in a field and leaving them to it, you know. They hate the wind and rain, for a start. They're not waterproof, and they like to keep warm and dry. It's all right for Fred, he's a hardy cob. He can happily stand under the tree or by the hedge, and the weather won't bother him, but it would be a nightmare for the goats. They need a proper shelter, preferably with a concrete floor and loads of straw to bed down in, and the fencing is going to have to be goat-proof, which isn't as easy as it sounds.'

Xander looked embarrassed. 'I'll pay for new fencing, and a shelter. I'm sorry. The woman who asked me to take them in didn't mention any of this. I just assumed they'd be outdoors grazing all day.'

'They're not grazers, they're browsers. They need plenty of roughage and a constant source of clean water. They won't drink dirty water, so we'll have to make sure it's checked and changed constantly. They'll need a hayrack, too. They get tangled up in nets. This is going to be a nightmare.'

'I knew you'd say something bad about them,' Sam muttered.

Rachel's heart sank. 'I'm just being practical, Sam. If you're going to have animals, you have to look after them properly.'

'Maybe we could tether them?' Her mother's voice was laden with disappointment.

Rachel tried to hide her irritation. It was all right for Xander and her mum, bringing all these animals to the farm, but they clearly didn't know that much about them. It was a case of heart-over-head, and Rachel was clearly more her father's daughter than she'd realised. She hadn't been aware until now of how much information she'd gathered, just by being around him. 'It's dangerous to tether goats. They'd end up strangling themselves. We'd be far better off putting them in the field at the back of the house, where we used to keep Milkmaid. Her old shelter's still there. I'll check it over, make sure it's in good condition. We can bring them into the barn every night, and keep them indoors during bad weather and throughout winter.'

'Who's Milkmaid?' Xander said, interested.

'Long story, and not worth telling,' she assured him.

Sam eyed her warily. 'So, are you saying we can keep the goats?'

'What else are we going to do with them? We'd better keep them in the barn for now, until we can get the field suitably fenced.' She gave Xander a warning look. 'It won't be cheap, though.'

'Whatever it costs,' he assured her.

'I don't suppose their owners even told you if they've been wormed, or treated for parasites?'

Xander had to admit no one had mentioned it. 'I shouldn't think they know, to be honest. The goats belonged to the woman's aunt, and she died. They sort of got landed with Mabel and Maureen.'

'The way we have,' she muttered. 'We'd better get Merlyn round to check them over. More money. Good job we have a CPH, although I don't suppose you even know what that is.'

Xander and her mother exchanged nervous glances. 'What is it?'

'County Parish Holding. All land that's going to house livestock has to have one. Are the goats tagged? Please tell me they're tagged.'

'They are, yes.' Xander looked relieved that he could say something positive at last.

'I'll have to report that the goats have been moved onto our land. I'll get on to that tomorrow.'

'What on earth for?'

Rachel sighed. 'They're livestock. It's the law.'

'How do you know all this?' Her mother looked quite astounded. 'You never wanted to be a farmer.'

'Maybe not,' Rachel said with a shrug, 'but that didn't stop me from helping Dad out around here. I picked up a lot without even realising it. He knew you liked goats, Mum, and he did look into it at one point, but he told me they were more bother than they were worth. He said they're greedy, boisterous, always escaping and getting into trouble, and under your feet.'

Her mother looked deflated and Xander looked mortified. 'Sorry, Rachel. I had no idea.'

'Clearly.'

'I'm ever so sorry,' Xander repeated. 'Maybe I should find somewhere else for them to stay for a week or so, until we get the fencing sorted?'

'They can't leave here now for six days. That's the law, too. Besides, what's the point? By the time you've found them somewhere to go, we can have the fencing erected. I know the company Dad always used. I'll get on to it tomorrow. I suggest the two of you go online tonight and try to find out as much as you can about keeping goats. I think you're both going to have a bit of a shock.'

'I would never have agreed if I'd realised how much work it would involve,' Xander assured her. 'Although,' he added, scratching his head thoughtfully, 'I don't think I actually did agree. I don't remember saying yes at all. It just sort of happened.'

'And still no company for poor Fred.' her mum said regretfully.

It was Rachel's turn to look sheepish. 'Actually, I may have got that covered,' she admitted.

'Oh?'

'Er, the fact is, we've got another guest arriving on Saturday — well, if I get the go-ahead tonight, that is.' Seeing their puzzled looks, she held up her hands. 'Okay, okay. I'm as bad as you. I couldn't say no, okay? We've got a pony arriving — an elderly chestnut called Ginger.'

'Ginger!' Her mum looked delighted.

'Fred and Ginger! How perfect!'

'Wow, a pony! This gets better and better,' Sam said, his sulkiness forgotten.

'Maybe you could learn to ride him?' Rachel said cautiously. 'What do you think?'

'Really? Oh, that would be ace!' Sam was practically hopping up and down in excitement. He grabbed Xander's hand. 'This is great, isn't it, Xander? Two goats and a pony coming to live with us. We're like a proper farm, almost, aren't we?'

'We are!' Xander grinned down at Sam and ruffled his hair affectionately. 'All we need now is a big shiny tractor and some chickens. What do you think?'

As Sam laughed, Rachel felt a tremor run through her. What was with the *we*? It was her mother's farm, not Xander's. Watching Sam beaming up at him, she realised that Xander had somehow become part of their lives, and part of the fabric of Folly Farm. Sam had clearly bonded with him, but what was the use in that? Xander was a famous actor who wouldn't be hanging around in Bramblewick for very long. She was going to have to make sure that Sam didn't get too attached to him — and, somehow, she was going to have to make sure that she didn't either.

12

Ginger, as it turned out, was a stocky little chestnut with a flaxen mane and tail, and a white blaze, half-hidden by a shaggy forelock almost as long as Fred's. She was brought to the farm by Francesca's grateful father, who couldn't hide his relief at finally having found another home for her.

'If Harriet hadn't moved away, maybe it wouldn't have come to this, but then again . . . Truthfully, I've been worrying about her for ages now, and Frankie is so stubborn, you see; but really, with her going to university, and me and the wife having no idea about horses and suchlike — well, at her age, what's the point of keeping her?'

Xander couldn't help but wonder if Mr Green would say the same about his own mother. He couldn't imagine parting with an animal friend simply because she was growing old. He supposed not everyone was fortunate enough to be in the position to keep them into old age. Mr Green's circumstances had clearly changed, from what Rachel had said about his working hours being cut, and who was he to judge? At least this chap had found Ginger a decent home, unlike poor Fred's previous owner.

'All her tack's there, along with grooming kit, paperwork, and some feed.' Mr Green opened his car door and nodded at the huge pile of equipment he'd dumped by the stable door. 'Farrier took her shoes off a couple of months ago when Harriet left, and we didn't bother replacing them. Frankie's been reading up on it — reckons horseshoes are cruel. I don't know. It's all beyond me, and to be honest, I'd rather be fishing. Oh well, thanks again for taking her off my hands.' He gave them a grateful smile and climbed into the car, slamming the door shut and starting the engine immediately, as if he was afraid they would change their minds and tell him to put Ginger back in the trailer.

As they watched his vehicle bumping out along the farm track, Xander and Rachel each let out a long sigh, then looked at each other and grinned.

'What have we done?' Rachel said, eyeing the pony, who was standing in the loose box being fussed over by Sam. They'd put plenty of fresh straw down as bedding, in preparation for Ginger's arrival, and she had a full hay net and a trough full of water. They planned to introduce her to Fred the following morning and, all being well, turn her out into the field with him. The fencing had been erected around the goats' field, and Mabel and Maureen were already making sure Fred knew he had neighbours. Fred was, luckily, a calm and steady sort of horse, and their frequent calls to him didn't seem to bother him at all. Hopefully Ginger wouldn't be upset by them either.

'What have *you* done, you mean,'

Xander said, raising an eyebrow. 'You can't put this one on me. Oh no. For once, I'm completely innocent.'

Janie laughed. 'Makes a change.' She nodded over at Sam. 'He looks very happy, though.'

'I know.' Rachel looked happy, too. 'I've spoken to the lady who runs the White Rose Riding School over at Kearton Bay. She's happy to teach Sam to ride. He's going to start lessons next Saturday.'

'I was thinking,' Xander mused, 'that maybe I ought to get some tack for Fred. Start riding him — with Merlyn's say-so, of course. It would do him good to get some exercise. Help build up his muscle tone.'

'You can ride?'

He looked quite affronted. 'Madam, I'm a crime-fighting earl. Of course I can ride.'

She giggled. 'Sorry, I quite forgot.'

'Janie filled me in on Milkmaid. It was quite an interesting story.'

Rachel pulled a face. 'I'll bet it was.

Best to gloss over that. Milkmaid and I didn't see eye-to-eye. I wasn't much of a rider, to be honest.'

'Maybe you could try again on Fred? I'd be happy to give you some refresher lessons.'

Rachel shuffled, clearly unsure. 'We'll see. Maybe you could give Sam some tips, though? It would be good for him to have someone to help him out between lessons, and perhaps you could go for a short hack with him one day, when he's ready.'

'I'd enjoy that. I think Sam would, too.' Xander tried not to think about the fact that he probably wouldn't be in Bramblewick by the time Sam was ready to go hacking with him. He glanced across at the young boy and smiled. 'He's good with animals, isn't he?'

'Do you think?'

Rachel's voice was loaded with tension, and he glanced at her, surprised. 'Don't you?'

'I don't know.'

'What an odd thing to say,' Janie said.

'Of course he is. Look how he's bonded with Duke. That dog's devoted to him. And Darwin's almost as fond of him as he is of you, Rachel.'

'How is Darwin?' The kitten had been at the farm for a whole month now, and had settled in beautifully. Clearly he was already part of the family, which wasn't surprising. Xander felt like part of the family, too. Folly Farm had that effect.

Rachel and Janie exchanged glances. 'Hmm. We had a bit of a shock yesterday,' Rachel admitted. 'At least, Mum did.'

'Oh? What happened?'

Janie wrinkled her nose. 'I found something rather nasty in his bed. Two toes. Bless him, they'd dropped off.'

'Oh, that's disgusting.' Xander felt vaguely nauseated. 'Did you take him to see Merlyn?'

'I rang him. Luckily, he was on his way home from a call out at the Twydales' farm, so he very kindly called in. He's not worried. Said he half-expected they

213

would come off on their own. There's no cause for alarm.'

'Is he getting around all right? Darwin, I mean.'

'Bunny-hopping. He's a determined little thing. Oh, Rachel, is that your mobile?'

Hearing her ringtone, Rachel pulled a face. 'Can't think who'd be calling me at this time.' She pulled her phone from the back pocket of her jeans and glanced at the screen.

Xander watched as her expression changed. Her face paled, and the hand holding her phone was definitely trembling. 'Er, excuse me.' Her voice was shaky, too. He watched as she walked away from them, head down, phone against her ear. Her whole demeanour had altered. Xander would bet his last pound that he knew who was on the other end of that phone call.

'Sam, are you going to say goodnight to Ginger now?' Janie's voice sounded too bright. Evidently she'd noticed the change in Rachel's manner too. 'You can help Xander and me put all this equipment in the old tack room. Come on.'

Sam reluctantly rubbed Ginger's nose one last time, then closed the loose box door behind him. He seemed quite keen to help, though, once Xander passed him the saddle to carry into the tack room. He was soon busily telling his grandma and Xander all about the riding lessons he was about to start, and how he planned to be the best rider ever.

'I can't wait for next Saturday,' he told them excitedly, as they put away the last of Ginger's belongings and locked the door.

Rachel was standing outside. 'We may have to change the date of your lesson.'

Xander turned, handing the tack room key to Janie as he kept his eyes on Rachel. She looked white. 'What is it?' he said gently.

'I don't want to change my lesson,' Sam protested.

'Thing is, Sam, that was your dad on the phone.'

Sam's eyes widened. 'Dad? Is he coming to see me?'

Rachel shook her head. 'No, but he wants you to go and see him. He wants you to stay with him for the weekend. How do you feel about that? You don't have to go,' she added hastily. 'If you'd rather stay here and take your riding lesson and — '

'I can go riding any time,' Sam said, evidently forgetting how important it had seemed just a few moments ago. 'I want to stay with Dad.'

'How's he going to get there?' Janie said, her hand on Rachel's shoulder.

'I said I'd meet Grant halfway between here and Leeds,' she replied. 'I'll hand Sam over and come straight home.'

Sam was overjoyed. 'I'll be able to ride my bike again, and I can see Kyle. He's my best mate at school,' he informed Xander. 'Oh, I can't wait! I'm going to tell Duke! Oh, can I take Duke with me?'

'I don't think that's a good idea,'

Janie said. 'Duke's very old and not well. It would be too much for him.' Seeing Sam's expression, she said, 'You don't want to make him really ill, do you?'

Sam sighed. 'No. Course not. I just wanted Dad to see him, that's all. You will look after him while I'm away, won't you?'

'Of course we will.' Janie smiled. 'Now, Sam, why don't you and I go indoors, and I'll make a start on supper while you feed Darwin and Duke? You're very welcome to join us for supper, Xander. Perhaps you and Rachel can shut Mabel and Maureen up for the night?' She gave Xander and Rachel a meaningful look and led her grandson back to the house.

Xander stuck his hands in his pockets, feeling awkward. 'I'm guessing this isn't good news.'

'The worst.' Rachel's eyes were brimming with unshed tears. 'I really hoped — I don't know what I hoped.' She kicked at a bunch of weeds sprouting out from a crack in the yard. 'I can't stop him from seeing his dad, can I? As much as I want to, it's not right, is it?'

Was she wanting his permission to do just that? Xander could hardly give it. He didn't know the ins and outs of the situation. He'd already formed an opinion of Grant Johnson, based on the fact that he'd happily drowned some tiny kittens, but other than that he didn't know much about him. When all was said and done, Sam was the man's son. If Xander had a son, it would break his heart if he never saw him.

'You know what's best for your own child,' he said finally. 'I'm sure you wouldn't do anything that wasn't in Sam's best interests.'

'You think?' She sounded bitter. 'You might be surprised.' She shrugged. 'Oh well, I guess I'd better ring Georgia at the riding school. Maybe Sam could be squeezed in early, before I have to drive him to York. That's where I'm meeting him. Not exactly halfway, is it? But the main thing is, of course, that it's more convenient for Grant.'

'Would you like me to go with you?' The words were out of his mouth before he'd even thought about what he was saying.

Rachel stared at him. 'Go with me?'

'For company, I mean. And moral support. Maybe — maybe we could go somewhere after we've dropped Sam off? York's a lovely city. We could spend the afternoon there, get something to eat?' His voice trailed off. 'Forget it. Sorry. Bad idea.'

He saw her swallow, watched nervously as she stood there, clearly trying to decide what to do for the best. Finally, she nodded hesitantly. 'Thank you. I'd like that.'

'You would?'

'Yes, honestly. If you meant it, I mean.'

'I meant it.' He really had, too. All right, he hadn't given it much consideration, but once the words were out, he'd thought that it was a pretty good idea. Rachel would need a distraction, and she'd need cheering up. Besides, the thought of spending an afternoon together, just the two of them, was surprisingly appealing.

'That's so kind of you. I'd only be wallowing all afternoon otherwise. Thanks, Xander.'

He smiled at her. 'You're very welcome, Rachel. It would be my pleasure. Honestly.'

For a long moment, they gazed at each other, then Rachel turned away. 'I'd better get the goats in. Supper will be on the table at this rate.'

'Gosh, yes, is that the time?' He glanced at his watch, not registering what it said at all.

'Are you joining us?' She sounded reluctant, as if she was only asking out of politeness. Xander wished he could fathom her out.

'It's all right. I need to get home after I've helped you with the goats. Belle and Rumpel will have their legs crossed,' he joked.

She laughed. 'Poor things. You'd better go then. I can manage Mabel and Maureen on my own. You don't want poodles in puddles.'

He liked to hear the sound of her laughter, but he felt sad at the relief in her voice. 'I don't mind helping. Another ten minutes won't make much difference.'

'Honestly, I'm fine. I don't want desperate dogs on my conscience.'

He managed to smile, somehow. 'Okay, if you're sure. Night then, Rachel.'

'Night, Xander.'

She was already walking away from him, and Xander stood for a moment, half-hoping she'd turn around and give him one of her too-rare smiles. When she disappeared around the back of the farmhouse, he sighed; then headed, rather confused, to his car.

13

Xander stayed in the car while Rachel took Sam to meet his dad. He half-wanted to go with them, curious to see the man who clearly caused Rachel such anxiety, yet had won her heart enough for her to marry him. In the end, though, he felt it would be better to stay out of the situation, unless Rachel wanted otherwise, which she clearly didn't. In fact, as she got back into the car after dropping off her son, she murmured, 'I hope Sam doesn't mention you.'

Xander looked at her, surprised. 'Why not?'

'Grant's a bit — ' She hesitated, then shook her head. 'It doesn't matter. It would just be easier all round, that's all.'

'But we're just friends,' Xander persisted. 'He can't object to you having friends, surely?' She'd needed a friend with her, and Grant must understand that. If he hadn't volunteered, Janie would probably have gone with her, but she'd been clearly relieved to discover Xander had already offered. It turned out that Jenna and Faye, who ran the dance school in Hatton-le-Dale, were starting dance classes for the over-sixties, and Janie and one of her reading group friends had decided to enrol, much to Rachel's astonishment. No doubt Janie would have put her daughter first, but there had been no need. Xander was more than willing to be a friend to Rachel.

'Forget it. I'm just being silly. So, here we are in York. What shall we do first?'

Xander frowned. 'How did it go? Really.'

She took a deep breath. 'Nerve-wracking, to be honest. I was dreading seeing him, and I was right to. He still has the same effect on me.'

He didn't want to ask what effect

that was. Did she mean she still loved her husband? That seeing him again had reminded her of that fact? He was shocked to feel an emotion bubbling up inside him that he'd never really experienced before — jealousy. Startled by its ferocity, he jammed on his sunglasses and baseball cap, and opened the car door. 'Come on, let's go sight-seeing.'

Rachel climbed out of the car and leaned against it, taking deep breaths. Xander, in spite of his churning stomach, couldn't help but feel sorry for her. 'Are you okay? It must be tough on you, seeing him again after all this time. Is there any chance — I mean, maybe you two could work it out?'

Her eyes widened. 'Me and Grant? You must be joking!'

He could feel the tension leaving him as she shook her head vehemently.

'It took me far too long to get away from him. Now that I have, I'll never go back. It's just — seeing him again. It turns me back into that stupid, scared coward. I feel ashamed all over again.'

'Ashamed of what?'

'Of putting up with him for so long. For staying put, lying to myself that it wasn't so bad, pretending that it was the best thing for Sam, when really the best thing for Sam would have been for me to be brave and take him with me as far away from Grant as I could manage.'

He hitched up his sunglasses to look at her properly. 'It was that bad?'

She was quiet, chewing her lip. Eventually, she lifted her face to meet his gaze. 'Worse. But let's not talk about that now. Let's just hit the shops, the museums, get something to eat. I want to see York. It's years since I've been here.'

He wanted to push her, to ask her what had happened, but he couldn't do that to her. Evidently, she didn't want to discuss the matter any further, and he'd promised her a good day out. He would make sure she got it. He smiled at her, putting his sunglasses back in place. 'Where shall we start?'

They decided to begin with York Castle Museum and take it from there. They'd only expected to spend an hour or so browsing the exhibits, but the place was so huge, and so packed full of interesting things, that they ended up staying there much longer.

Rachel lingered far too long for Xander's liking over the historical clothing on display. She got a fit of the giggles when she spotted an eighteenth-century gentleman's costume. 'Is this the sort of thing you wear? When you play Lord Curtis, I mean.' At least she said it in a whisper, so the people around them didn't hear.

Xander rolled his eyes. 'Similar. Okay, you can laugh now.' He was a bit taken aback when she did. 'How rude. I'll have you know, I look very dashing.'

'Do you wear the wig, too?' she added, nodding at the white hairpiece propped up behind the glass case.

Xander actually felt himself start to blush. 'Sometimes,' he admitted. 'Only on special occasions.'

As she let out another peal of laughter, a bubble of joy seemed to rise up inside him at the sound, and he found himself laughing with her. 'I don't care what you say, Mr Darcy has nothing on Lord Curtis,' he assured her, tongue firmly in cheek.

Xander took off his sunglasses as they wandered around the mock-up of dark Victorian streets, peering into shop windows and eyeing lines of laundry hanging between the 'buildings', before popping into the 'Victorian school-room'.

'Reminds me of my school,' Xander grumbled. 'It's enough to give me nightmares.'

'Your school?' Rachel nudged him. 'How old are you?'

'It was a public school,' Xander said, as if that explained everything. 'Firmly rooted in Victorian values, too. We didn't get the cane, but it was very strict. I hated it.'

'Was it a boarding school?'

'It was, but I was close enough to go

home every weekend.'

'Then what was the point of being a boarder?'

Xander shrugged. 'All part of the experience, I suppose. And it was childcare for the parents.'

'Oh.' Rachel sounded subdued. 'How awful.' She linked her arm through his. 'I'm so sorry.'

At her touch, Xander felt as if an electric charge had just shot through him. 'It's fine,' he managed, with a half-laugh. 'I survived. And look at me now. It's one of the sweetest pleasures in life that I actually have more money than my own father. He was convinced that I was a disaster waiting to happen. Sent me to a school that concentrated on mathematics and science in a bid to make me forget all about this *play-acting nonsense*. Of course, he quite forgot that at university I would find plenty of outlets for my creative ambitions, and lots of like-minded people. I did well at school, just as he'd demanded, but it backfired on him.'

'Fancy trying to force your child to give up something he loved.'

'He wanted me to do what he did. He's a financier. He thought actors were doomed to poverty — and to be fair to him, most of us are. It's only down to a massive stroke of luck that I'm not signing on for benefits right now.'

'And to your talent.' Rachel squeezed his arm. 'My dad always hoped I'd take over the farm, but when I didn't want to, when I told him I wanted to be a nurse, he never tried to persuade me otherwise. He supported me, whatever it was I wanted. I was very lucky.'

'I'm sure you'll do the same with Sam,' he said.

'Of course. Yes.' She sighed. 'I'm hungry. How about you?'

He realised she was thinking about her son and his father again. Time for a change of scenery. 'Lunch? And then some shopping?'

'Shopping? What sort of man are you? I've never met one yet who wanted to go shopping!'

'I'm a gentleman,' he reminded her. 'This is your day out, and if you want to go shopping, that's what we'll do.'

They found a pretty little café off the beaten track down a cobbled side street. Sneaking into a secluded table at the back of the room, Xander sat facing the wall, while Rachel faced the other diners. She looked around and then grinned at him. 'It's okay. No one's taking any notice of us. You can take them off now.'

Relieved, he removed his sunglasses and put them on the table. 'Sorry about all this,' he said. 'I just don't want us to be disturbed.'

'It must be a total pain,' she said. 'How do you have any sort of normal life at all?'

'But I do, really,' he assured her. 'To be honest, you can make it as normal as you choose. Well, within reason. I don't do the showbusiness scene. I hate it. I have to go on promotional tours, of course, and appear on chat shows and the like, but other than that, I tend to stay away from it all. I don't like parties and premieres. I'd much rather be at home with my dogs and a good book.'

'You must be unique,' she mused.

'Not at all. My friends are just the same. Do you remember me telling you about the friends who live in Kearton Bay? Well, they're very similar. Joe, especially. Joe Hollingsworth, you know?'

She nodded. 'I remember Joe. Used to be a chat show host, didn't he? He had those micro pigs that were on his show every week.' She tutted. 'I wasn't impressed with that, encouraging too many idiots to buy animals they had no idea how to care for.'

'He still has them. To be fair to Joe, he didn't buy them. They were a gift; and, having got them, he's done his very best for them. They live with him on a small farm, and they're not exactly teacup size anymore.' He grinned. 'Joe's with Charlie Hope now — you know, the comedian? — and they're as domesticated as you could hope to be.

Joe's retired from showbusiness. He writes novels. I don't think Charlie will give it up for years — he loves it so much — but he told me how happy it makes him to go home and live a low-key life in the village. All the villagers know they're there, but no one bothers them. They're just accepted. They're so lucky.' He sighed. 'That's the kind of life I'd love.'

'What? You'd give up the acting?'

He shook his head. 'No. I don't think I'd ever do that. It's all I ever wanted to do. But that balance, the best of both worlds. Acting in stuff you really care about, then going home to peace and quiet and beautiful countryside and your animals. What more could you want?'

'Nothing, I suppose, when you put it like that,' she murmured.

It was on the tip of his tongue to add that the only thing that could be more perfect would be to have what Joe and Charlie had — someone to come home to. Someone to love. Someone to love him. But he didn't dare put that into words. She might be frightened off, and that was the last thing he wanted to do. He picked up the menu, suddenly brisk. 'So, is there anything that you fancy?'

She visibly gulped, and they stared at each other for a moment over the menus. Xander's heart thudded. What was that look she was giving him? It seemed to call to something inside him — some part of him that recognised it and responded in kind. Then she jerked her gaze away from him and the moment was over.

'The warm goat's cheese salad with onion marmalade sounds nice.' She seemed pretty doubtful as she said it, and he arched an eyebrow.

'Really?'

She pulled a face. 'No, not really. I was trying to sound posh, what with you being a famous actor and an ex-public schoolboy.'

'You must be joking!' He scanned the menu then tapped it triumphantly.

'That sounds more like it. Giant Yorkshire pudding with sausage, mash and gravy. Now that's what I call a lunch.'

'Lunch? More like a hearty supper.' She grinned at him. 'Are you really going to eat that? It sounds very filling.'

'Good. I'm starving. What about you?'

'The toasted cheese and tomato sandwich, I think.'

He rolled his eyes. 'Don't go too mad, will you?'

'You know what Mum's like. She'll have a massive tea waiting for me tonight. I can't eat too much now.'

He nodded. She was quite right. 'What about a drink?'

'Just a cup of tea for me,' she said.

'Same here.' He put down the menu, decision made.

Rachel leaned over. 'Waitress heading over,' she murmured. 'You might want to put your sunglasses back on.'

'I'll just keep my head down,' he whispered.

He could feel the waitress hovering by his side as Rachel reeled off their order, and felt rude at not acknowledging her presence, but it just wasn't worth it. He knew, only too well, how easily one person's recognition could lead to a mini-stampede and the ruination of a perfectly pleasant day. Although he liked to downplay Bay Curtis's popularity, the truth was that there were hordes of besotted fans out there. He knew of at least two dozen Facebook groups that had been set up in appreciation of either himself or his character, even though he wasn't even on Facebook and never responded to anything posted about himself on social media. His co-stars often laughed when he admitted he'd never even joined Twitter. They seemed to spend most of their time between takes updating their accounts, tweeting non-stop and posting photographs to Instagram. It made him shudder. Although, one cynical actress had told him that his refusal to play the fame game probably only added to his appeal. 'There's an air of mystery around you,' she said. 'With so many actors these days, we even know what they had for breakfast. You don't play by the rules, and so you're intriguing. People can't get enough of you. Wise move, Xander. Well played.'

But he wasn't playing anything. He thought about Joe and Charlie, tucked happily away at Whisperwood Farm. They had the life he craved. Peace, rural surroundings, the careers they wanted, and each other. Perfection. For a moment, he allowed himself to daydream, imagining himself appearing in the theatre, taking a bow to thunderous applause, feeling the excitement and adrenaline rush from playing to a live audience, heading back to Bramblewick afterwards. Heading back to Folly Farm. To Rachel . . .

'Thank you so much.'

He blinked, realising that the waitress had returned with their pots of tea. 'Thanks,' he said gruffly, hoping his voice was well-disguised. The waitress didn't seem to notice him anyway. She gently put down the cups, assured them their meals wouldn't be long, and left them to it.

The food, when it arrived, was good. They ate, drank, and chatted throughout, mostly discussing the animals and how they were doing. Xander tried hard to steer the conversation away from Sam; and, when they'd exhausted the farm, he asked her about her work.

'I haven't been there long, obviously, but I'm settling in well. They're a lovely bunch of people. At my last place, the doctors were grumpy old devils, but Connor and Riley are lovely. Then there's Anna, who's Connor's wife. Her dad used to be the village doctor. Connor took over after he died — that's how they met. It was quite romantic, actually. And then there's Holly.' She smiled. 'Holly's a real character. She has no tact, but she's got a heart of gold, and she's so funny. I'm really fond of her. I'm really fond of them all.' She looked thoughtful. 'I've been very lucky. It's a great place to work.' Then she wrinkled her nose. 'It will be even better when all the building work's finished.'

'What are they having done?' Xander scooped up the last of the mashed potato with some regret. 'It looks like a construction site from the side.'

'A new consulting room for a third GP, bigger waiting room, extension to the main office. It will be great when it's finished, but it's a real pain at the moment.'

'That's quite an extensive build.'

'Yes, it is. They've been waiting for planning permission for months, though, and they're really excited about it. Did you know, last year there was a real danger that the surgery would be closed down? Can you imagine?'

'No, I can't. Clearly there's been a complete turnaround in that little plan.'

'Absolutely. Luckily for me, they decided to expand instead.' She considered for a moment. 'It's going to be amazing when we have three GPs. They're talking about training either Anna or Holly in phlebotomy, too, so if I'm fully booked up, one of them can take bloods. There's a little room off the main office that can be converted for that purpose. It's going to be great. Just getting through the mess and noise for the next three months or so, that's the problem.'

He saw the gleam in her eyes and realised she loved nursing as much as he loved acting. They were both lucky. They'd found what they wanted to do with their lives. How many people could say that?

Rachel insisted on paying for lunch, which went against everything Xander stood for. He felt distinctly awkward as she handed over her credit card at the counter, while he sat there feeling like a heel. 'It just doesn't feel right,' he moaned as they headed back into the street.

'Don't be so old-fashioned,' she said. 'You paid for us to go to the museum.'

'Quite right, too,' he grumbled. He wanted to protest that he had far more money than she did, but didn't feel that would go down too well. 'This is all wrong.'

Rachel tutted. 'All right, Lord Curtis, if it's that impossible for you to cope with, you can buy me a coffee when we've been round the shops.'

He brightened. 'Sounds like a plan. Where are we going?' He indicated a large, rather grand building at the end of the street. 'I suppose you'd like to walk round there.'

Rachel followed his gaze. 'What is it? Oh, Rochester's? Not really. I'm not a department store sort of girl, even if it's as posh as that.' She beamed at him. 'Shall we go to The Shambles?'

'I've never been there,' he admitted. 'I've heard of it, though. If that's what you want, that's fine by me.'

He loved this side of her. In spite of the fact that she was clearly still anxious about Sam being with his father, she was definitely excited about being in York. She'd thoroughly enjoyed going around the museum, and the prospect of visiting this medieval street was obviously delighting her, which delighted him.

Upon reaching the celebrated street, he began to see why she'd been so eager to visit. It was pretty much how he'd imagined Diagon Alley in the Harry Potter books. In parts, the ancient buildings leaned towards each other, reaching across the cobbled street, their roofs almost meeting.

'It's the oldest street in York,' Rachel told him. 'And the most-visited street in Europe.'

Xander wasn't sure if she was joking or not, but he wouldn't be surprised if it was true. The fifteenth-century buildings were charming beyond words and, despite the heaving crowds, he didn't feel as if he was in any danger of being recognised, because the street was so pretty that people were absorbed in taking in every last detail of it — far too busy to notice some actor walking amongst them, baseball cap pulled down tightly on his blond head, and sunglasses firmly in place, hiding those famous blue eyes.

'It's lovely,' he breathed, peering

through one of the quaint little shop windows. 'So charming.'

'It is now,' she told him. 'It wouldn't have been so charming a few centuries ago. Livestock was slaughtered here, and there were loads of butchers on this street. See how the pavements are raised up? That's 'cause all the blood and guts used to get washed away along these channels by the butchers. Not really the place for an animal lover.'

'You have to spoil the illusion,' he said. 'I imagined this street as some sort of gathering place for witches and wizards in days of yore, purchasing their newts' eyes and frogs' toes.'

'Seriously?' Her eyes widened, and he laughed.

'No, not seriously.'

'You may be able to buy those things now, though,' she said, her cheeks turning a rather fetching shade of pink. 'There are a few Harry Potter shops here. I haven't been in them, but I imagine they're very popular. It's said that The Shambles was the inspiration for Diagon Alley, you know, so I'll bet the shops are a real tourist magnet.'

'And full of movie fans.' He shrugged. 'Probably best for me to avoid it, if you don't mind. I'm happy to wait outside if you want to go in.'

'No, it's fine. Lots of other things to look at.'

They wandered down the street, soaking up the atmosphere, popping into the odd shop, peering through the windows. There was a penny press machine dispensing special York coins, and a shrine to the Catholic saint Margaret Clitherow. After admiring some jewellery made with Whitby jet in a shop window, Rachel had to physically stop Xander from heading inside to buy it for her.

'You don't have to buy me anything. Stop being so pushy.'

'I feel I owe you,' he admitted.

'For what?'

'For all the extra work I've dumped on you. Mabel and Maureen, for a start. I had no idea they took so much care and attention, and I know you're not keen on goats. I'm suffering from a severe attack of guilt.'

She wrinkled her nose. 'Can I tell you a secret?'

'Of course,' he replied, surprised.

She leaned towards him and whispered, 'I've changed my mind. Naughty and nosy they may be, but Mum was right. They're adorable. So full of personality, and so affectionate. I've quite fallen in love with them.'

'Really?'

'Really. So, you see, I don't need anything from you to say sorry. Now, stop feeling guilty and put that credit card away.'

Reluctantly, he gave in, and they headed into a little café and had a coffee each, before heading back to the car park.

'I've had a lovely day,' Rachel told Xander, as they finally pulled back into the yard at Folly Farm. 'Thank you so much for coming with me, and for taking my mind off everything. You really didn't have to do that.'

'I wanted to do that,' he assured her. 'It was my pleasure. I've had a lovely day, too.' The engine was still running. He wasn't sure if he was invited in or not. Maybe she'd had enough of him for one day. 'I wonder how your mum got on at the dance class. Do you think she coped with it all right?'

Rachel giggled. 'I think the question is, did the dance class cope with Mum all right?' She leaned back in her seat, looking relaxed. 'It's so good to see her getting out and about again. She's a different woman these days, what with dancing and the reading group. Did I tell you Merlyn's started taking dance classes, too?'

He couldn't imagine it, no matter how he tried, but he was quite glad to hear it all the same. 'He and your mum are very good friends.'

'And getting friendlier all the time.' She smiled fondly at the thought, then glanced across at him. 'It all started with you, you know.'

'Me?' He was puzzled. 'What did I do?'

'When you brought Fred to us, it seemed to change everything. I don't know.' She shook her head. 'Things just seemed to move forward after that. Mum brightened up so much, and Sam — Sam seemed to show a different side to himself. A softer side.'

'And what about you?'

'Me?'

He swallowed, suddenly nervous. 'Did anything change for you when I brought Fred here?'

She was watching him, seeming unable to reply. He saw the crimson flush on her cheeks, the slight parting of her lips, the innocence in those big, dark eyes. Before he knew what he was doing, he leaned over and his lips pressed against hers, his hands cupping her face. His heart thumped in his chest as she hesitated for a moment, then responded. The adrenaline rush was bigger than anything he'd ever experienced, even in front of a live theatre audience. He'd never had this physical and emotional reaction to a kiss before

— not even with Martine, and he'd been engaged to her. Breathlessly, he pulled away from Rachel and stared at her. What was she doing to him?

'Well,' she murmured, 'that was unexpected.'

'Was it?' He stroked her face softly. 'You must have felt something this afternoon, surely? Hasn't this been building for some time?'

She chewed her lip, the way she did when she was thinking. 'You're a very good actor, Xander.'

He shrank back, stung. 'You think I'm pretending? That this is some sort of game?'

She unclipped her seatbelt, gathering her bag from the footwell. 'No, I'm not saying that.'

'Then what are you saying?'

She opened the passenger door. 'Just that. You're a very good actor. And I'm a very good nurse. Thank you again, Xander. I really appreciate what you did today — taking me to York, I mean. Bye.'

He opened his mouth to speak, but realised he had no idea what to say. What was she talking about? He unclipped his own seatbelt, meaning to go after her, but then paused. He knew Rachel well enough by now to know when she needed to be left alone; and right now, she needed to be left alone. Whatever was going on in her mind, she needed space to fathom it for herself. He, meanwhile, had plenty of thinking of his own to do. He fastened the seatbelt again and drove slowly out of the farmyard, wondering what on earth he was going to do next.

14

Rachel's stomach churned as Grant's Mercedes pulled up in the York car park. She'd spent the entire weekend telling herself that everything would be fine — that Sam would be the same little boy who'd left her on the Saturday morning, that Grant couldn't affect him that much in just two days. Even so, as she climbed out of her car and watched her son and estranged husband walking towards her, she realised her legs were shaking. Could Grant have possibly undone all the good that Folly Farm seemed to have achieved in such a short time?

Sam waved to her and began to run. The delight in his face at seeing her was a huge comfort. At least Grant hadn't managed to poison him against her — not this time.

'Mum, Mum, I've had a great time!

And you'll never guess what!'

'All right, Sam, give your mother a chance to breathe.' Grant's voice was smooth and calm, but his hand was firm on his son's shoulder. Sam quietened immediately. Rachel wasn't surprised. Grant had that effect on people. Even so, it infuriated her. She wanted to tell Sam to shout his news out from the rooftops, just to spite his father. She didn't, though. She knew better than that. Grant was smiling at her now, a smile that was firmly restricted to his mouth, while his eyes watched her shrewdly. 'I've been hearing all about your venture at the farm. Sounds quite amazing — all those waifs and strays.'

Rachel felt a lump in her throat. 'Shall I take Sam's bag?'

Grant made no move to hand it over. 'Dogs, cats, goats, horses. Quite a menagerie. And I hear you've adopted another stray — some actor or other.'

Rachel's hand stretched out to Sam, but he was just out of reach, and firmly in the grip of his father. He stared up at her, a look of confusion in his eyes. She gave him a wide smile. 'So, you had a great time, eh? That's wonderful. We've missed you, though — me and your grandma. And Duke can't wait to see you.'

'Has he been all right?'

'He's missed you, but he's fine. You can tell him all about what you've been up to when you get back. Do you want to say goodbye to your dad now?'

Sam moved forward. Grant let him go, but he was still holding the bag. 'Who's Duke? Is that the actor?' He gave a sarcastic laugh.

'You know Duke.' Sam frowned. 'I told you all about him. He's my dog.'

'Oh, the old dog.' Grant shrugged. 'You haven't told your mother your news yet, Sam.'

How could he? You made sure he didn't. Rachel longed to say the words out loud but didn't dare. 'Can I take his bag?' she asked again.

It was as if she hadn't spoken.

'Sam, tell her about your present.'

Sam looked uncertainly at Rachel. 'Dad bought me a puppy.'

Rachel felt the bile rise in her throat. 'A puppy?' She stared at Grant. 'Why would you do that?'

'Why shouldn't I do that?' His tone was challenging. He was in the mood for an argument, she could sense it.

'Where — where is he?'

'She. She's at our house. Where else would she be? It *is* our home, after all.'

'Was. It's your home now.' She tilted her chin, trying to sound calm. She hoped he wouldn't see that she was trembling.

'We'll see. We called the puppy Rachel, didn't we, Sam? A tribute to you, my dear.' He smiled, the insult clear. 'Anyway, the puppy's staying with me. I think you have enough animals to deal with at that rundown farm of your mother's, don't you?'

Rachel took hold of Sam's hand. 'Come on, Sam. We've got to get home. It's getting late.'

'So, who's the actor?'

She heard the edge to his tone and knew he was masking a seething anger. 'Just someone staying in the village who loves animals. He didn't have room for them, and we did. End of.'

'End of? He seems to spend a lot of time at the farm.'

How much had Sam told him, for goodness' sake? Rachel was silent, knowing that if she said the wrong thing it would be a spark to the tinder.

'Well?'

'I told you. He's just an animal lover with nowhere to keep animals. He's only on holiday in Bramblewick. He won't be around much longer.'

'I'm very glad to hear it.' Grant didn't even blink as he kept his gaze on her. 'I'm not sure I want that sort of person hanging around my wife and child.'

Rachel's heart pounded as she waited, not daring to move. After what felt like forever, Grant suddenly smiled and handed her the bag. 'See you in a couple of weeks, Sam.' He ruffled his son's hair and Rachel let out a breath, feeling dizzy. 'I'm away next weekend,' he told Rachel, 'but I'll take him the weekend after that.' It wasn't a request.

Rachel clutched the bag to her chest like a shield. 'Ready, Sam?'

Sam nodded and headed towards the car, Rachel following him, her legs feeling distinctly unsteady.

'See you soon, Sam,' Grant called. 'And don't worry. I'll look after that cute little puppy for you. I'll soon have Rachel well-trained.'

Rachel almost dropped her car keys as she fumbled with the remote, feeling sick. She had to get out of there — away from Grant's menacing presence, and back to the comfort and safety of Folly Farm.

★ ★ ★

Xander found his steps slowing as he reached the track which led to Folly Farm. Beside him, Rumpel and Belle pulled on their leads, eager to explore. They recognised the place, clearly, and their enthusiasm was heartwarming. He wished he could share it.

It had been just short of two weeks since he'd last seen Rachel. Oh, he'd visited the farm almost daily to check on the animals, chatted with Janie, even stayed to see Sam on a couple of occasions. He'd always made sure, though, that he timed his visits for when Rachel was at work.

It wasn't that he didn't want to see her — quite the contrary, in fact. He wanted to see her so badly it hurt. He physically ached for her. He'd replayed that kiss over and over in his mind, and he longed to repeat it in real life. The trouble was, she clearly *didn't* want to repeat it, and that hurt more than he knew what to do with.

Xander didn't think he was a vain man, nor was he stupid. He knew he was lusted over by countless women, but he was sensible enough to realise that it had nothing to do with who he really was. It was just an image that his fans had formed of him. They didn't know him. Most of them had never seen him in the flesh, and never would. It was Lord Bay Curtis, with his perfectly-styled hair, made-up face, dashingly-dressed form, and carefully-scripted lines, who had won their hearts; not Xander South, a man who was happiest in jeans and wellies, tramping the countryside with his dogs.

Lord Curtis would have known what to say to Rachel, no doubt. He'd have impressed her with his witty banter, flashed that winning smile, dazzled her with his bravery and charm. Then again, he thought that someone like Rachel wouldn't be in the slightest bit interested in a man like Bay. Maybe that was what attracted him to her so much. Rachel was extraordinary in her very ordinariness. As someone who spent most of his time around fellow actors, her dedication to nursing, to motherhood, to her own mother, was wonderfully refreshing.

Life with Rachel could be perfect, he thought. Not flashy, not glamorous in any way, but perfect all the same. He knew she would make him happy. The question was, could he make her happy? Was he good enough for her? Or would his fame, his career, drag her down with him, spoil the lovely little life she was busy creating for herself and her family?

He wasn't sure of the answer, so he'd stayed away, giving them both time to take in what had happened between them. From his own point of view, the voluntary separation had been hugely beneficial. He knew now exactly what it was he wanted, and he'd finally contacted Penny and put the wheels in motion, much to her relief.

'I suppose it's something, at least. Well done, darling. You know it makes sense. I'll contact Grayson and get back to you. He'll be thrilled, I'm sure.'

Grayson had wasted no time getting back to Penny, and now things were moving at a frantic pace, just as he'd feared they would. Yet, in a way, he was also glad. Nothing could stay the same forever. His holiday in Bramblewick was almost over — quicker than he'd expected, but that was a good thing. He'd got what he had come for, after all. Time to move on. Now he just had to put it to Rachel. He needed her to know that he wasn't acting when he was around her, that every word he told her was genuine. Would that be enough for her, though? He just didn't know.

He knocked hesitantly at the farmhouse door, knowing that it would be Rachel who answered. Janie had already told him that she would be at the reading group that Friday night, and that Sam was going to Grant's straight from school.

Grant was coming closer, agreeing to collect Sam from Malton. Soon, he might even venture as far as the farm. That would be interesting, he thought, feeling that now-familiar pang of jealousy towards the man who had stolen Rachel's heart. Who was this person who'd managed to make her fall in love with him, married her, fathered a child with her, and then thrown it all away? Whoever he was, he was an idiot, which was some small comfort.

Rachel opened the door, and her face coloured when she saw him standing there. He realised he was smiling at her like some gormless fool and tried to make his face behave. She looked so pretty standing in the doorway, her hair loose, face makeup-free, cheeks pink with embarrassment. Or was it the shock of seeing him?

'Xander! This is a surprise.' She stared at him for a moment, then shook her head. 'Sorry, come in.'

Pulling the door wide open, she stood aside to let him in, bending to pat the heads of Belle and Rumpel. 'It's been a while,' she said, closing the door behind them. 'I was beginning to think I'd done something wrong.'

'Of course not.' He unclipped the leads from the poodles' collars, then straightened, meeting her gaze head-on.

'I thought — I thought after what happened, I should give you some space.'

The pink spots on her cheeks deepened and spread. She gave a half-laugh and turned away, heading into the kitchen. 'What happened? Oh, I see. For goodness' sake, Xander, it was just a kiss. It didn't mean anything.'

He followed her, determined that she wasn't going to fob him off. Not this time. 'Now who's acting, Rachel?'

Her back was pressed against one of the kitchen units, her hands gripping the worktop at either side of her. Her face looked as if it had been scorched. 'What's that supposed to mean?'

'Rachel, please.' He took hold of her hands and held them to his chest. 'Let's not play these games any more. You must know how I feel about you.'

'Why must I?' Her voice sounded choked. 'I'm not psychic, you know.'

She was right, he realised. He'd never told her, not really. He didn't have the easy manner, confidence and way with words that his alter ego had. Bay would have bombarded her with words of love, but Xander didn't quite know how to express the whirlwind of emotions that was assaulting him.

'It's all new to me,' he said suddenly, almost panicky. 'How I feel, I mean. I've never — I mean, I don't know how to tell you. I've never been in love before.'

Rachel gently removed her hands from his grasp. 'You were engaged,' she reminded him. 'Please don't insult my intelligence.'

'I'm not! It's my own intelligence I'm insulting — my emotional intelligence, at least.' He gazed at her, anguished. 'I really believed I loved Martine, you see.'

'Martine! That was her name!' Rachel blushed again as he stared at her in surprise. 'Sorry. We were just trying to remember — me and the girls. We knew you'd been engaged to her, but we couldn't — it doesn't matter.'

So, they'd been talking about him?

And about his engagement, too. Was that a good thing or a bad thing? He wasn't sure. This wasn't going as well as he'd hoped. When he'd played this scene out in his imagination, many, many times, she'd fallen into his arms the moment he told her he loved her, but evidently it wasn't going to be that easy. 'Er, yes, well, I did get engaged to her, and I truly thought it was love. When she broke it off, she told me it was because I didn't have the commitment to her that I should have. I thought she was being too needy, to be honest. I had no idea what she was talking about.' He shook his head. 'I'm quite ashamed of myself, Rachel. I didn't know what love was. Not until I met you.'

She was watching him, her face expressing nothing. He floundered, not knowing what else he could say to convince her. 'This is coming out all wrong,' he admitted. 'I sound like a fool. Pathetic. What more can I say to convince you that I love you?'

As she continued to watch him, it

occurred to him that perhaps it wasn't words that were needed. Taking a leaf out of Bay's book, he moved towards her and kissed her — very gently, very carefully, terribly afraid that she would push him away. He was delighted and thrilled, therefore, when she kissed him back, quite desperately. The blood stirred in his veins, and he pulled her to him, revelling in the joy of her response, which seemed to be as fevered as his own.

Eventually, they pulled apart and stared at each other, their breathing heavy, eyes wide. Xander ran his hand through his hair. 'That was — wonderful.'

'Yes, it was.' Rachel looked rather dazed. 'How inconvenient.'

'Inconvenient?' He felt a sickening lurch of dread. 'What do you mean?'

'Xander, it's pretty obvious that we're attracted to one another. There's no point in me denying it. You're a very good-looking man, and more than that, you're kind and compassionate and sweet.'

'Thank you. I think.' He felt bewildered. Where was this conversation going? He had an awful feeling it was heading in a direction he didn't like.

'I could easily fall in love with you, Xander, but where would it get me? No, please just listen.' She held up her hand as he started to protest. 'We're worlds apart. You're a famous actor. You live in a completely different world to the one I inhabit. I don't want to be stuck here in Bramblewick, reading about what you're up to in the newspapers or magazines, only seeing you if I subscribe to Netflix. That's no life for me, and our relationship would never survive.'

'But it doesn't have to be like that,' he said desperately. 'Remember what I said about Joe and Charlie? They make it work!'

'Charlie's a top comedian, but he doesn't go off to America to promote his shows or films, does he? And he's hardly going to have women — I mean, men — throwing themselves at him. No offence to Charlie, I'm sure he's lovely, but he's not exactly a heartthrob, is he?'

'You mean you don't trust me?'

'How could I blame you? Surrounded by all those glamorous actresses. What on earth would you want some dowdy nurse for?'

Xander tutted, exasperated. 'You're not dowdy! You're beautiful. And if I wanted some glamorous actress and that kind of life, what am I doing here in the depths of the North York Moors, spending every spare moment I have on a farm, moping around after you?'

'Moping around?' She gave him a suspicious look.

'Yes, Rachel. Moping around. Do you think I can concentrate on anything else? Don't you know you're all I think about, all I want? I love you and I want to be with you, here at Folly Farm. Nothing else matters.'

'So, you're not taking that Hollywood film? Or doing another series of the show?'

He swallowed, dropping his gaze. 'Well, yes. I mean, the thing is — '

'There you go, then.' She reached over to where the dog leads were lying on the worktop and picked them up. 'Here you are,' she said, handing them to him. 'Please don't make this any harder than it needs to be, Xander. Let's at least part on friendly terms.'

'I don't want to part at all! If you'd just listen, you'd understand. I turned down the film role. I don't want to be in Hollywood, that became very clear to me.'

'So, you're returning to play Bay Curtis?'

'Yes — but Rachel, it's the last time, I swear. I've spoken to the producer and, thank goodness, we're on the same page with this. We both think the show is running out of steam, but I've agreed to do one last series to tie up all the loose ends and give the character the romantic ending the fans are craving.' He gave her a faint smile. 'Everybody loves a happy ending, and even Lord Curtis deserves one.'

'When does it start filming?'

'September. But — but I'm going away on Monday.'

She shrugged. 'Okay. Going where?' Despite her casual demeanour, he could hear in her voice that she was choked, which gave him fresh hope.

'London. I've accepted the role in the play, and we start rehearsals next week. Four weeks rehearsing, then tech week, then a five-week run. It'll be over by mid-July, though, so it won't clash with filming. Of course, there's a chance it will go to the West End after that, but if it does, it will be with someone else in the lead role.'

'I see.'

'Do you? Do you really? Because what I'm trying to explain is that, after I've finished with Lord Curtis, I'm going to concentrate on theatre work. Hopefully, doing plenty in the north. And I want to be based here, in Yorkshire. With you.'

Rachel bit her lip.

'Rachel?' He hooked a finger under her chin and gently tilted her face so that she was looking directly at him. 'What do you think?'

'I think — ' She took a deep breath, 'I think it all sounds lovely for you, and I'm glad you've decided to follow your heart. I wish you well with your acting career, Xander, I really do. But it doesn't change anything between us. I don't want to be an actor's girlfriend. I'm still married, in case you'd forgotten, and I'm trying to build a new life for myself and for Sam. I don't need the distraction. Please try to understand.'

He felt as if a concrete slab was sitting in his chest. 'You're serious, aren't you?'

'I'm afraid so. Now, could you please leave, because I'm actually having supper at Holly's. I wasn't going to, but she persuaded me; and really, it's the best thing for me if I'm going to build my life in this village, isn't it?'

His mouth opened and closed wordlessly. 'I guess so,' he managed eventually. He took the leads from her hand. 'I'll leave you in peace, then.'

He clipped the leads back onto the dogs' collars and headed, feeling numb, towards the door.

'Xander!'

He turned, a dart of hope piercing his heart for just a moment. She was staring at him, her face pale, her eyes large and dark. 'I'm sorry.'

'Yeah.' He gave her a faint smile. 'Me, too. Bye, Rachel.'

15

It was Izzy's birthday, and Rachel was cordially invited to a late and leisurely lunch at The Ducklings, Nell's home. Nell, apparently, was preparing a meal for them all; and, as everyone raved about Nell's food, Rachel was sure to have a good time — according to Anna and Holly, at least.

Anna, in particular, was insistent that Rachel tag along. 'You'll only be sitting at home all alone if not. Come on, it will be a laugh.'

Since she couldn't deny that she would be alone, Rachel gave in and agreed to go. Sam was at Grant's again, and Janie was attending a meeting of her reading group, before heading off to Helmston for lunch with some members of her dance class — including, no doubt, Merlyn. She was a different woman these days, quite her old self, and Rachel was delighted to see her regain her old spark and zest for life. It was just a bit dispiriting to realise that she herself had no life whatsoever, outside of work. She knew she had to try to build up her own network of friends, and maybe tagging onto a ready-made group was the easiest solution. It wasn't as if she didn't already feel very fond of Holly and Anna. It was more that she felt particularly uncomfortable around Izzy.

As Sam's teacher, Izzy was all too aware of what had happened with the little boy in the dinner queue, and Rachel was ashamed. She was also — although she didn't acknowledge it even to herself — worried that Izzy might have more to tell her. Had Sam done anything else recently? Would Izzy announce it to the entire group over lunch?

Rachel wouldn't dwell on such matters, and tried to look forward to the meeting as she knocked on the door of Nell's little cottage, The Ducklings, which was a pretty little stone building overlooking the beck.

'Come in, come in. You're just in time. I'm taking the last of the quiches out of the oven.' Nell beamed at her and Rachel smiled nervously.

'Quiches, plural? How many people are coming to this lunch?'

Nell looked puzzled. 'Only the usual gang. Five of us. Come on, in you come. Isn't it warm outside? I've got all the windows open and it's still hot in here. Talk about flaming June.'

Rachel followed her through to the kitchen where Anna and Izzy were perched on stools, glasses of orange juice in hand.

'You made it! I'm so glad.' Anna pushed a glass of juice towards her. 'Here, drink this. It's freshly-squeezed, and just the job on a day like this.'

Rachel took it with thanks, slipping onto a stool beside Anna. 'Happy birthday, Izzy,' she said, sliding over a birthday card and a box of chocolates. 'No Holly?'

'Oh, thank you very much. Holly's on her way. Knowing her, she's at Maudie's right now, frantically looking for a decent birthday card for me,' Izzy said, her eyes crinkling with amusement. 'Always last-minute, is our Holls.'

'No wonder she didn't fit in at the chemist's,' Nell said, pulling on oven gloves and heading to the cooker. 'Can you imagine someone so disorganised working in a place like that?'

'No worse than her working in a doctor's surgery,' Izzy pointed out, pulling the card from its envelope and smiling approvingly.

'Hmm, except there she didn't have me to cover for her, hurry her along, or shut her up when necessary, did she?' Anna laughed. 'Bless her. I do love her, though.'

Nell opened the oven door and pulled out a tray bearing two quiches. 'There we are. That's the last of them.'

Izzy shook her head. 'You're not feeding the five thousand, you know.' She grinned at Rachel. 'Thanks for the

card, Rachel, I love it. And those chocolates are my favourites, although after
what Nell's made for us, I can't imagine
being able to eat for weeks. You should
see the dining table. It's positively groan-
ing with food. I hope it doesn't end up
in the bin.'

'Oh, don't worry about it,' Nell assured
her. 'Whatever's left over, Riley will scoff
tonight when he comes round.'

'Riley doesn't live here, then?' Rachel
queried, sniffing appreciatively as Nell
carried the quiches past her.

'Golly, no. Not yet, anyway. He lives
in the flat above Spill the Beans. We've
only been going out together for six
months,' Nell said.

'No wedding bells on the horizon for
you then? Shame. I'm thinking it's time
this village had another wedding. I
really enjoyed the last one.' Izzy winked
at Anna, while Nell looked appalled.

'You know perfectly well that neither
Riley nor myself are keen on weddings.'
She put the quiches onto her granite
worktop and stepped back to admire

them. 'If we ever do get married, we'll slip away to a registry office and no one will be any the wiser until we get back. You and Matt can have the big wedding, though. Nothing stopping you.'

'Except he hasn't asked her.' Anna laughed.

Izzy tutted. 'As if that would stop me. If I wanted to get married, *I'd* ask *him*. That's a long way off. I'm far too young to get married.'

'Thirty-one today,' Anna reminded her. 'Clock's ticking.'

'Oh, shut up. I'm still a spring chicken.'

The front door banged shut and Holly rushed in, red-faced. 'Sorry I'm late. I got delayed.' She shoved a carrier bag on the worktop and plonked herself down on a stool. 'Orange juice? You must be joking! Where's the champagne?'

'There is no champagne,' Anna said firmly.

Holly reached inside the carrier bag.

'Oh well, at least I brought this.' She pulled out a bottle of Prosecco and a card. 'Happy birthday, Izzy.'

'You left the price on the card,' Nell said. 'Just come from Maudie's, have you?'

Seeing Holly's embarrassed expression, they all laughed. 'Told you!'

Izzy didn't seem in the least bit put out. 'Get the glasses, Nell!'

'Not for me, thanks.' Anna shook her head as Nell pushed a glass in her direction.

'What? Are you mad? It's my birthday. We've got to celebrate.' Izzy grabbed the bottle from Nell and began to fill Anna's glass, but Anna was having none of it.

'Sorry. I'm sticking to orange juice today.' She cleared her throat. 'And for the foreseeable future.'

There was a silence as her words sank in, then Nell squealed. 'Oh my word! You're pregnant!'

Izzy's mouth dropped open. 'Pregnant? How did that happen?'

'Get Rachel to tell you, she's a nurse,' Holly said.

'I mean, I didn't know you were trying for a baby so soon.' Izzy stared at Anna. 'I can't believe it.'

'We thought we might as well start trying as soon as we got married,' Anna said, her eyes sparkling with happiness. 'Gracie's already nine, and we thought that was a big enough gap; though, to be honest, we're a little surprised it happened so quickly.'

'When's the baby due?'

'December. I didn't want to say anything until we'd had the first scan, but I had it on Friday, and it's all going beautifully.'

'So that's why you were so late on Friday morning,' Holly said. She clapped her hand to her forehead. 'Morning sickness! No wonder you were so ill for a couple of weeks back in April. And there was I, blaming myself for giving you a stomach bug.'

'Sorry about that, Holls.' Anna sounded genuinely apologetic. 'I wanted to tell you, but I was scared. It was too soon. You understand?'

'Of course.'

Rachel held up her glass. 'Congratulations, Anna. It's wonderful news. I'll bet Connor's delighted.' She took a sip of her wine, pushing away the memory of the day she'd told Grant she was pregnant. *Delighted* wasn't the word that sprang to mind there.

'He is.' Anna hesitated. 'He's a little worried, too.'

'What about?'

'I think he's concerned that Gracie won't react well to having a baby brother or sister. It's all unexplored territory, you see.'

'Gracie tends to surprise us all,' Nell said reassuringly. 'She might adore it from the off.'

'I hope so. You know Connor. He's always worrying that I've taken on too much with Gracie. His ex-wife leaving because she couldn't cope has left him with anxieties. I think he's imagining the worst — that, if Gracie doesn't bond with this baby, it would put too much pressure on me and I'd go, too.' She sighed. 'Somewhere inside him, he knows it wouldn't happen. I'd never leave him or Gracie, never mind my own baby, but I guess some wounds go deep.'

Rachel took a gulp of wine. That was true enough. Some wounds, it seemed, never healed.

As the five of them headed into the dining room a short time later, the discussion was still firmly centred around Anna's news. Nell produced another bottle of wine from the fridge and poured Anna a glass of lemonade. Poor Izzy's birthday seemed to have been well and truly forgotten.

'Connor's a wonderful father,' Anna said, helping herself to some salad. 'He's going to be lovely with this baby.'

'I'd hate to have a baby with a doctor,' Holly mused, waving a half-eaten sausage roll in the air. 'Such know-it-alls. Imagine it. He'll be telling you during every stage what's happening to you, and you won't get the chance to play on it and exaggerate all your twinges because he'll know you're having him on, so you'll never get him to run around after you while you lie on the sofa, telling him you can't cook the tea because you're pregnant.'

They all stared at her. 'I really pity the bloke you end up with, Holls,' Izzy said eventually. 'Poor fella. What a life he'll lead.'

'I think Riley will make a lovely father,' Nell said dreamily. 'He's really fond of kids, and he comes from a big family. All his brothers have children, and Riley keeps in touch with all his nephews and nieces. Always remembers their birthdays and stuff. He's so sweet.'

'Ugh. How nauseating,' Izzy said. She helped herself to a slice of quiche and looked over at Rachel. 'Of course, you're the only one of us who knows what it feels like — to go through pregnancy, I mean.'

'Ooh, yes.' Anna prodded a tomato with her fork and stared eagerly at

Rachel. 'What's it really like?'

'And does it really hurt as much as they say?' Holly said. 'You know, giving birth? Because it looks absolutely horrific in the films.'

'Thanks for that, Holls.' Anna tutted and turned back to Rachel. 'How was it for you?'

Rachel was on her third glass of wine. She was finding all this talk of pregnancy and romance far too painful. Her own pregnancy had been a nightmare of trying to keep Grant placated, make sure he didn't feel neglected, assure him that he was still the most important person in her life. She'd spent the entire nine months practically ignoring the fact that a baby was on the way, frantically ensuring that she didn't get too much attention.

She remembered the day her colleagues at her old practice had turned up unexpectedly at her house, gifts and cards in hand, all eager to celebrate the rapidly-approaching birth. It was her first week of maternity leave and she was a nervous wreck. Grant had come home early. He'd been all smooth charm to the girls, but she'd recognised the signs. Sure enough, as soon as they left, he'd raged at the mess, banged doors, thrown his dinner at the wall, then spent the next two days sulking. He didn't like it when the attention was on her.

'It was okay,' she said finally. 'Textbook, really.'

Nine days in hospital because her blood pressure had shot up. No wonder, really. She'd been so stressed out and exhausted, trying to carry on as normal, making sure the pregnancy hadn't affected Grant's comfort in any way. They'd induced in the end, worried about her health. Sam arrived ten days early after a pretty horrific labour. Grant hadn't stayed for the birth. He'd hung around for a few hours, but then pointed out that he had to be at work the following morning and needed his sleep. She'd been quite glad to see him go, although the midwife had looked appalled. No need to tell them all that, though.

'And does it really hurt that much?' Holly enquired, helping herself to pasta. 'Only, I always think all that screaming and grunting they do on the telly must be a bit over-the-top.'

Rachel drained her glass. 'Every woman's different,' she said, not wanting to scare Anna by telling her how truly awful it had been for her. 'You can't generalise. Besides, there are epidurals if it gets too bad.' And didn't she wish she hadn't left it too late to ask for one!

'I want a natural childbirth, if possible,' Anna said.

Rachel rolled her eyes. They all said that until the contractions started.

'I don't get the whole natural childbirth thing,' Nell said. 'I mean, all that pain, for what? You wouldn't have a natural appendectomy, would you?' She shuddered. 'I was glad to be put to sleep when they took my appendix out, I can tell you.'

'Removing an appendix isn't the same as removing a baby!' Izzy giggled. 'It's a wonder of nature. A miracle. Of course you want to feel it.'

Nell and Holly gave each other knowing looks. 'I want the works if I ever have a baby,' Holly said. 'In fact, they can just knock me out and wake me up when it's over. Good luck, anyway, Anna.'

Anna looked a bit pale at all this debate. Izzy patted her hand. 'Take no notice. Just think, when it's done, you'll have a gorgeous little baby in your arms. Do you want a boy or a girl?'

Anna brightened. 'I really don't mind. It must be lovely to see him or her for the first time.' She smiled over at Rachel. 'What does it feel like, Rachel? To meet your child, I mean?'

Rachel had just started on her fourth glass of wine and was feeling distinctly light-headed. 'Fabulous,' she said gaily. 'Best feeling in the world.'

'Was your husband with you?'

Rachel's smile dropped. 'Nope.'

'Oh. Didn't he want to be? Or did he not make it in time?'

Rachel should never have had so much to drink on so little food. She knew, even as she told them what had happened at the hospital, that she would regret it, but for some reason, her mouth wouldn't stay shut. It all came pouring out: Grant's resentment that a baby was on the way, his lack of care or concern for her, his couldn't-care-less attitude at the hospital — and, worst of all, his complete disinterest in his son when he finally arrived.

'He only really started to pay attention to Sam when he was old enough to be manipulated. Then the games began. *Let's see how much we can turn him against Rachel. Let's make Rachel the bad one, the boring one, the one who spoils all the fun. Let's see how easily I can break Rachel's heart.*'

She slammed her now-empty glass down on the table and glanced up at them. They were all staring at her in shocked silence. Rachel felt sick, and it wasn't all down to too much alcohol. 'Did I say all that out loud?'

'Oh, Rachel.' Anna shook her head, her face stricken. 'I'm so sorry. I had no idea.'

Rachel swallowed. 'Why would you? I should never have said anything. I'm sorry.'

'He sounds like an absolute pig,' Izzy murmured.

'That's being polite,' Nell said. 'You poor thing.'

Rachel gritted her teeth. 'Please don't say that.'

'But it must have been horrible for you,' Holly said, her eyes glinting with tears. 'I'm really sorry, Rachel. I feel so bad for you.'

Rachel pushed her plate away. 'Stop saying that! Don't you think I've had enough of being *Poor Rachel*?' She glared round at them all, barely registering their shocked expressions. 'Years and years of being *that woman*. The one to feel sorry for. The one they talk about in hushed tones. The one whose bruises they pretend they haven't noticed. The one who says she's accident-prone but they all know what's really going on, and isn't she stupid to stay with him, and how selfish to leave her child in that sort of environment, and really, doesn't she deserve everything she gets? Even so, *Poor Rachel!*'

She rose, and stumbled out of the room into the kitchen to find her bag. She needed to go home. She'd known it was a mistake to come here today. She simply wasn't in the mood, what with Sam staying at Grant's, no doubt being drip-fed his poison, and Xander gone . . .

She wondered, for a moment, how he was getting on. Mrs Lovelace had re-let Sweet Briar Cottage. She'd seen a young couple coming out of there, hand in hand, all set to explore the moors in the early summer sunshine. The sight of them had overwhelmed her with sadness and a sense of loss. She missed Xander more than she'd ever imagined she would. She knew she could have found out how he was doing if she'd tried. There would be reviews of his play, no doubt. She could Google him, and he'd be right there on the screen in front of her eyes, but she didn't want to know. Not really. She was too afraid what else she might discover. Just how happy was he to be back in London? Besides, she didn't think she could stand to look at his face. The longing for him was just too much to bear.

'Oh, Rachel, don't. Don't.'

Rachel wondered what Nell was talking about, until she started to dab at her face with tissues. Then it dawned on her that she was crying, and she wondered when that had started. She stood, allowing her friend to wipe away her tears, aware that the others were standing in the doorway watching, then Nell's arms went around her, and she wept freely — for letting Sam down, for all the pain she'd endured from Grant, both physical and emotional, for her cowardice and her weakness, and for the loss of a man who had done nothing but love her. It was comforting to be in Nell's embrace, but there was no mistaking the fact that it was Xander's embrace she craved. But that would never happen again. She'd pushed him away. How could she do anything else? Loving Xander would only lead to pain. For her, for Sam — and for Xander himself. She had to be strong, for all their sakes.

16

Janie peered out of the kitchen window. 'Looks like Rachel's home with Sam.' She turned to smile at Xander, who was standing pale-faced by the table, holding Darwin. 'Don't look so scared. I'm sure she'll be thrilled to see you.'

Xander wasn't so sure. It had been almost three months since he'd last seen Rachel, and they'd had no contact since the day he'd walked away from her, back at the end of April. He'd half-decided not to return to Bramblewick. He had a life in London, after all. The dogs were settled again in his apartment, the final series of *Lord Curtis Investigates* was on the horizon, and he'd been looking at various scripts and offers that Penny insisted on sending him.

The truth was, though, he couldn't concentrate on anything. He had committed to the last series of his television show, but beyond that, he had no plans — and found that he rather liked it. He wasn't worried, despite Penny nagging him. He could never spend the money he had already earned, and he'd made some sound investments over the years. Maybe that was part of the problem. He wasn't hungry for success any longer. He wasn't hungry for fame. A different hunger burned in him now, and it was making it impossible for him to think about anything else.

After lecturing himself for being a coward, Xander had made the decision to give it one last shot with Rachel. If nothing else, he wanted to see how Darwin, Duke, Fred, Ginger, Mabel and Maureen were doing. He'd transferred a large sum of money over to Janie's account before he left, in spite of her protests, so he knew financially they would be okay. If they'd needed veterinary treatment, there would be no problem. Even so, he'd like to see for himself if they were still happy and thriving.

He'd missed Janie, too. She was a quite remarkable woman, and Xander had grown very fond of her. And Sam was a cute kid who'd been through some tough times. He knew Rachel worried about him and, having all this time away from the family, he'd had plenty of opportunity to put the pieces of the jigsaw together and make a good guess why. Little hints she'd dropped about bad influences around Sam, the way she'd flinched when he'd grabbed her arm that day, her aversion to, and fear of, male aggression, her desperate desire to keep Sam away from his father . . . It made Xander sick to his stomach, but he had a pretty good idea that Rachel had been through some bad times with Grant Johnson. How bad, he wasn't entirely sure, but he had an awful feeling that she'd suffered physically as well as emotionally, and the thought of it broke his heart.

Sweet Briar Cottage was let, and

there'd been nothing else available in the area, which wasn't surprising given that it was now July and the holiday season was in full swing; but Joe and Charlie had welcomed him to Whisperwood Farm, and Kearton Bay wasn't too far from Bramblewick, so it had solved his problem. He'd been there a few days and Joe was already fed up with him moping around the farmhouse, too nervous to do what he'd gone there to do.

'Good grief, Xander, just man up and get it sorted. The girl obviously means the world to you, so what are you waiting for? Better to find out where you stand. Just get it over with, for goodness' sake.'

'You never know,' Charlie added. 'She might be pining away for you. She'll probably swoon when she sees you on her doorstep. Aw, it'll be proper romantic.'

Xander doubted it. Rachel wasn't the swooning type. She was more likely to demand that he go back to London and leave her in peace.

'But if you don't ask, you'll never know, will you?' Joe had a point, so Xander had finally climbed into his car after saying an apologetic goodbye to Belle and Rumpel, having decided they would be too much of a distraction this time, and headed along the moorland road towards Bramblewick.

He hadn't been at all surprised when Janie welcomed him with open arms — Janie was always welcoming, after all — but after all that build-up of tension, he'd felt deflated to discover that Rachel wasn't in. 'She's gone to York to collect Sam. She should be back in an hour or so. Have a flapjack.'

He'd felt too sick with nerves to eat, as delicious as Janie's baking was. Instead, he'd sat with her, fussing over Darwin and stroking a contented-looking Duke, listening to her fascinating tales of the reading group and dance class, while his stomach whizzed around like clothes in a spin dryer, and his heart thudded every time he heard a noise outside.

When Rachel's car finally did, unmistakably, pull into the farmyard, he'd leapt to his feet, as if looking for an escape route. Darwin had been most put out, and Xander hastily told him he was sorry and soothed his indignant little form while staring at the back door as if a demon was about to burst through it.

In the event, it was Sam who stormed into the kitchen, his mouth tight, his eyebrows knitted together in a deep frown. He didn't even acknowledge Xander's presence, but headed straight into the hallway and up the stairs.

'Good grief, what's wrong with him?' Janie turned back to the door as Rachel finally entered, head down, posture slumped. 'Rachel? What's up with Sam?'

Rachel looked up, catching sight of Xander, and looked shocked. She dropped her car keys on the table and stared at him, her dark eyes looking enormous in her pale face. 'When — when did you get here?'

'About an hour ago.' His voice sounded croaky and he cleared his throat. 'How are you, Rachel?'

She looked bewildered, as if she had no idea how to answer that. Janie repeated her own question. 'What's up with Sam?'

Rachel stared at her for a moment, as if trying to process what had been said. She sank into one of the chairs. 'I have no idea. He's been like that since I picked him up. Something went on at Grant's, but I don't know what. Grant was behaving very oddly, and Sam couldn't wait to get away from him. He'd clearly been crying. I think — I'm scared — ' She slumped down in the chair and gave a little shake of her head. 'I don't know.'

Janie and Xander looked at each other. He saw the steely expression in her eyes, and wondered how much she actually knew; or if she was, like him, just making guesses from the little clues Rachel had left.

'Do you think Grant's hit Sam?'

Xander's mouth dropped open. *Wow, just come out and say it, Janie!* Then again, if there was the slightest possibility that was true, he wanted to know it too.

They both watched Rachel as she suddenly went very still. For a long moment, there was no movement, and no one spoke. Darwin wriggled in Xander's arms, and he bent down to put him on the floor. They all watched him bunny-hop over to a sleeping Duke and curl up beside him on his blanket.

Rachel gave a strangled moan. Both Xander and Janie were beside her in a second. 'You *do* think it, don't you?' Janie's voice was laden with emotion as she put her arm around her daughter. 'Oh, Rachel. What did he do to you?'

Xander couldn't speak. He sat down in the chair next to Rachel's and watched as she took a deep breath. 'I'm so sorry, Mum. I couldn't tell you.'

'But why not? Do you think I didn't guess? I know I didn't see much of you, but that doesn't mean that when I did I didn't notice the marks on your arms, the bruises on your face that you'd tried to cover with makeup.'

Rachel bit her lip and Xander had to physically force himself to remain still. The desire to punch something out of sheer rage and frustration was coursing through him. It was an entirely new feeling, and he hardly thought it would endear him to her, given her fear of aggressive behaviour.

'It was more the emotional abuse,' she said eventually, her voice barely above a whisper. 'Yes, he did hit me sometimes, but I sort of dealt with that. It was the mental cruelty that nearly finished me off. The way he played mind games with me, twisted every-thing around so that I was always in the wrong, tried to convince me I was going mad. And Sam — '

'He hurt Sam?' Xander's throat felt tight with emotion. He could barely get the words out.

She shook her head. 'No. I never saw him hit Sam. I would have left immediately if he had. It was just — Sam was picking up on his behaviour, copying him. Grant had no respect for me, or for any woman, and Sam was learning that. They both started to turn on me, mock me. Sam always blamed me for everything. I was just the miserable one, the one who stopped him doing anything fun. Like not getting a dog.' She looked at them both, tears brimming in her eyes. 'Sam was always begging me to get him a puppy, but I wouldn't. Of course, Grant told him it was because I was a killjoy. Grant didn't want a puppy either — he hates animals. But it was much more fun to pretend that he did and watch Sam's resentment building. How could I trust Grant with a puppy when he drowned those kittens?' She turned a pleading gaze on Xander. 'You understand, don't you?'

His hand covered hers. She was icy cold. 'Of course I do.'

'But now Grant's bought him a puppy, and I'm really scared he'll get fed up with her and do the same to her.'

Janie looked distraught. 'He drowned kittens?'

'It was years ago, Mum, but yes he did. He's a warped and twisted individual. I should have left him years ago, but I never had the nerve. I kept telling myself that it was for Sam's good, that he needed to be with his father. Truth is, I was too frightened to leave. I don't trust Grant. He scares me to death, even now. But then Sam started to get into trouble at school. He bullied a little boy, and he was repeating stuff he'd heard Grant say. I thought, if I didn't get him away, he'd grow up to be just like his father, and I couldn't stand that.'

Janie was openly crying, and Xander tried hard to stay calm. The last thing either of them needed was for him to lose his cool. 'That's why you were anxious about him being around animals. I saw it in you. You were worried about him with Duke and Darwin, and you seemed so relieved that he took to them and was kind.'

'And that's why you let Duke sleep on Sam's bed.' Janie mopped up her tears. 'You must have been glad to see that side of him emerging. But, Rachel love, you must know that Sam's nothing like that man. He's a good lad with a kind heart.'

'He was in real danger of becoming cruel, Mum. I saw it in him. Not to animals — I never saw that, thank goodness — but he got in bother at his old school, and then again here. And he could be very scathing about me and my job.' She shrugged. 'He thinks nursing's basically handing out medicine and sticking a bandage on someone. His dad's job, on the other hand, well — ' She rolled her eyes. 'He's a financial whizz-kid and worthy of respect.'

'He's just a child, Rachel,' Xander said gently. 'He'll come to realise the truth. He's a decent boy, and things will come right.'

He realised his hand was still covering hers. She looked down at it but made no move to extricate it from his grasp. Was that a good sign? He hoped so, but he didn't think now was an appropriate time to pursue the matter. There were more important things to worry about.

'Do you really think Grant may have hit Sam this weekend?' Janie's voice was soft, but her eyes betrayed her anger.

'I honestly don't know. I tried to get him to talk to me all the way home, but he wouldn't. I don't know what to do. If Grant has hit him, I don't want him anywhere near Sam again; but if Sam won't tell me, what do I do about it?'

Janie and Xander eyed each other worriedly. 'Do you think he'd tell me?' Janie said.

Rachel sighed. 'I seriously doubt it, Mum.' She paused, then looked up at Xander. 'He might tell you, though.'

'Me?' Xander raised an eyebrow. 'Why would he tell me?'

She gave a bitter laugh. 'You're a man, for a start. He might trust you more. And he bonded with you. Before,

I mean, when you used to be around a lot. He really took to you. I think he might be more inclined to confide in you.'

'You think?' He felt ridiculously flattered and sort of warm inside that she thought that.

'Worth a try,' Janie said, nodding at him. 'And there's no time like the present.'

Xander took a deep breath. 'Okay. Which way to his room?'

17

Xander knocked softly on the bedroom door. There was no answer at first, then a choked voice said, 'Go away.'

'Sam, it's me. Can I come in?'

There was a silence for a moment, then some shuffling sounds before the young boy replied, 'S'ppose so.'

Xander pushed open the door and peered round. Sam was sitting on his bed, legs crossed, pulling absent-mindedly at the arm of a shaggy brown teddy bear. He'd clearly been crying. His little face was red and blotchy, and his eyelids were swollen. Xander's heart melted. He stepped inside, closing the door behind him. 'Do you mind if I sit down?' he said, indicating the bed.

Sam shrugged. 'If you like.' He glanced down at the teddy bear and threw it to the end of his bed. 'He's just from when I was a baby,' he said hastily.

Xander picked the teddy up. 'I still have my teddy bear from when I was little,' he admitted. 'He's not as smart as this little guy — quite tatty, in fact, and one of his eyes is missing, but sometimes, only a teddy bear will do.'

Sam looked doubtful. 'You have a teddy bear?'

'Sure I do. Doesn't everyone? He knows everything about me. You can trust a teddy bear with all your secrets, right?'

Sam's bottom lip was thrust forward in a pout. 'I guess.'

Xander leaned back against the bedroom wall, fluffing up the teddy's fur. 'He's in very good condition. You've taken good care of him.'

Sam was silent, staring at his hands, which were now plucking at his duvet cover.

'What's his name?'

'Huh?'

'The teddy bear. What's his name?'

'Oh. Bruno.'

'Bruno.' Xander grinned. 'Good

name for a bear.'

'My dad named him. He named all my toys. I don't know why.'

Because he's a total control freak, thought Xander grimly. He wondered how he was going to approach the subject of Sam's recent visit to his father without scaring the boy off. It was going to be pretty hard to talk about Grant Johnson without letting slip how much he loathed the man.

'Dad named my puppy, too.'

'Oh? What sort of puppy is it?'

'A cocker spaniel. Dad called her Rachel.'

Xander stared at him. 'Your puppy's named after your mum?'

'I suppose so. Dad seemed to think it was funny. I'm not sure.'

'No. Right. Well . . . ' It was clear to Xander that Grant was sending a message to Rachel, and the thought made him clench his fists in anger. 'Not a great name for a dog, is it?'

'No, it's awful.' Sam reached over and took the teddy bear from Xander's hand. 'But she's a lovely puppy. So cute.'

'I'm sure she is.' Xander smiled, then the smile slid from his face as Sam looked up, his face streaked with tears which were now running unchecked down his cheeks. 'What is it, Sam? What's happened?'

'He kicked her.' Sam clutched Bruno to his chest, his tears dampening the bear's fur. 'Rachel, I mean. He kicked her really hard because she'd chewed one of his shoes. I told him, that's what puppies do, but he wouldn't listen. She's just a baby, isn't she? He shouldn't hurt her like that, should he?'

'No, Sam,' Xander said grimly, 'he really shouldn't.'

'She was crying, and he wouldn't let me go to her.' Sam's words were gasped out between sobs. 'And he's been mean to her before, lots of times, shouting at her and stuff, but I didn't think he'd hurt her. But then this programme came on the telly, and you were in it, and I told Dad and he got all angry and he was swearing and saying bad things about Mum, and then he saw what Rachel had done and went mad. What if she chews something else while I'm here? What if he kicks her again, or worse? She'll be crying and crying, and I won't be there to help her.'

Xander held out his arms and Sam crawled towards him, resting his head on Xander's chest. 'I wanted to bring her back with me, but he said no. I don't know why he won't let me have her here. He doesn't like her, I can see that he doesn't, so why does he have to keep her at his house? And I kept asking and he got really mad and he said she was going nowhere and if I didn't shut up whining he'd get rid of her for good. He won't sell her, will he?'

Xander's mind raced. Who knew how Grant planned to shut the puppy up for good?

'She was lying on a blanket in the back seat of the car when Dad brought me home, and she was so quiet and didn't jump about like she usually does.

Maybe he's really hurt her. What can I do, Xander? Dad said I hadn't to tell Mum, or there'd be trouble, but I'm frightened something bad will happen.' He swallowed. 'I don't like Dad very much anymore. He's scary.'

'Okay, Sam, calm down. Let me and your mum take it from here, okay?'

Hope flared in Sam's eyes. 'Can you go and see him? Can you get Rachel back for me?'

Maybe he shouldn't make promises he couldn't keep? Maybe he would only let the boy down, make things worse. But as he looked into Sam's desperate face, Xander simply couldn't help himself. 'I'll get her back for you, Sam. You can count on it.'

★　★　★

'He did what?' Rachel's eyes sparked with anger. 'I'll kill him.'

'Not if I get my hands on him first,' Janie assured her. 'I've never heard the like of it, although why it surprises me,

I can't imagine. Not after hearing what he did to those kittens — and what he's been doing to you over the years.'

'But what do we do?' Rachel turned anguished eyes on Xander. 'How do we get Grant to give us the dog? I know him. He won't just hand her over.'

'I promised Sam I would get her back,' he confessed. 'I have to try.'

'You mean, go to Leeds? Confront Grant?' She shivered, clearly scared. 'You don't know him.'

'No, I don't. But I know of men like him.' He folded his arms. 'I won't let Sam down, Rachel. You can argue all you like with me, but I'm going to Leeds. I have to do this. God only knows what that poor little puppy's going through. I can't just leave her there with him.'

'But he'll want to know what it's got to do with you.' She looked scared to death. 'He's already been asking questions. He doesn't know who you are, but he does know there's been some actor hanging around. He's asked me every time I've seen him if you've been in touch. It wouldn't surprise me if he's pumping Sam for information, too.'

'Why would he do that?' Janie said.

'He still considers me his property,' she said, not meeting Xander's eyes. 'He wasn't happy to know you were coming to the farm. If you turn up at his house, demanding the puppy for Sam, he'll be furious. It could get really nasty.'

'I'll have to take that chance,' Xander said. 'Besides, he knows who I am now. Apparently, I was in some programme they were watching earlier, and Sam made the mistake of telling him it was me. I think that's what sparked the puppy incident. I have a feeling he was itching to give me a good hiding, but the poor little pup had to bear the brunt instead.'

'But you're not a fighter!' She grabbed his arm. 'You said so yourself. You can't fight your way out of a paper bag. Those were your words. You'd have no chance against him, and I couldn't live with myself if anything happened to you.'

His eyes narrowed as he surveyed her, seeing the fear in her eyes, hearing the tremor in her voice. A seed of hope took hold inside him, a tiny shoot of excitement sprouting up as realisation began to dawn. 'Rachel, is that why you sent me away that night?'

She let go of his arm, gazing up at him wordlessly.

'I'll just go and . . . yeah.' Janie shuffled out of the kitchen, Darwin in her arms, leaving them staring at each other.

'I thought you didn't feel the same way about me,' Xander said, his eyes never leaving Rachel's. 'I thought it was all about my career, and you not wanting to get involved with anyone after Grant, but it wasn't that at all, was it? You were trying to protect me.'

'You really don't know how scary he can be,' she said, shivering. 'When he loses it — I don't want you on the other end of his fist, Xander. And it's not just you to consider.'

Xander squeezed her hand. 'I promise you, I'll never let him touch you again.'

'You can't promise that! And there's Sam, too. He has contact with him regularly. Can you imagine if you were living here? Can you imagine how Grant would push him for information, and how he would lose his temper when Sam told him what was going on? He'd lose it. He'd make Sam pay. I can't trust him. And you can't protect us when you're halfway around the world filming some movie or other, can you?'

'I told you, I don't want to be halfway around the world. Oh, sweetheart, don't you believe me? I said I wanted to make Folly Farm my home, and I meant it. I want to be here, with you, with your mum and Sam, and our little menagerie of animals. I want to restore the farm, make all the repairs that are needed around here, teach Sam to ride, have a life. We could be so happy together. I'd like to do theatre work, sure, but mostly in the north. I don't need to earn money any more, and I don't crave fame. It's the pleasure of acting I love, it always was. I don't want to be a star, Rachel. I want to be a husband. Your husband.'

His hand stroked her cheek and he felt her start to relax against him, saw the tension seep from her face, the look of hope — and, oh, without doubt, longing — in her eyes. Her lips curved into a smile. 'I love you, Xander.'

He started to tell her that, yes, he loved her, too, but instead he decided to explain it all with a kiss. He'd missed her so much, and the warmth of her body against his as her mouth pressed against his own was enough to drive all thoughts of her vile ex-husband from his mind.

'Xander! Rachel!' Janie burst into the kitchen and they pulled hastily apart. 'I'm sorry to interrupt, but you'd better get ready for action. Grant's just pulled into the yard.'

There was a loud banging on the farm-house door. Rachel recognised the shape of her estranged husband through the frosted glass pane and her heart seemed to fly up into her throat. 'Go into the living room,' she urged Xander. 'Quickly!'

'You must be joking.' He shook his head and took hold of her hand. 'It's okay, Rachel, don't panic. I'm not going to let him touch you.'

It was very sweet of him, and quite courageous really, given that he'd admit-ted he was no fighter, but he hadn't seen Grant in a temper. He hadn't seen Grant full stop. She would have very much liked to keep it that way, but evidently, Xander had no intention of hiding.

Janie opened the farmhouse door and stepped hurriedly out of the way as Grant barged past her, dragging a blue roan cocker spaniel puppy in his wake. 'Come in, why don't you?' she muttered, clos-ing the door behind him.

'I knew it!' Grant stood quite still, staring contemptuously at Xander — who was still, Rachel suddenly realised, holding her hand. 'All that stuff about him going away. I knew Sam was lying. I might have known *you'd* lie, but to get him to cover for your tawdry little affair!'

'Don't you dare!' Feeling Xander's hand in hers seemed to give Rachel courage. She stood straight and tall, glaring at Grant in disgust. 'Don't you dare judge me by your low standards. I have never asked Sam to lie for me. There was nothing to lie about. Xander *has* been away, and only came back today. And there's no affair — tawdry or otherwise.'

'Not that it's any of your business,' Xander added smoothly. 'After all, you and Rachel have been separated for some time. Who she sees is up to her.'

Grant seemed taken aback at their defiance. 'She's my wife, in case you'd forgotten.'

'Not for much longer,' Xander assured him.

Rachel saw the flash of anger in Grant's eyes and her legs trembled. Xander squeezed her hand reassuringly, and she found the courage to speak. 'If you hadn't put so many obstructions in the way, we'd have been divorced months ago. I don't know why you're bothering, Grant, because the divorce will go through. You can't stop it.'

'Really? Well, maybe I should file a counter-suit. It's quite clear that adultery has been committed. Maybe I should name you in the petition. How would that go down with your millions of adoring fans, *Mr North?*'

'You'd have to prove it first,' Xander said calmly, 'and you'd have one heck of a job doing that, seeing as it's not true.'

'Sure it isn't,' Grant said, his face white with fury. 'We'll see what the solicitors make of this, shall we?'

'Rachel!'

They all turned as Sam rushed into the kitchen and threw his arms around the little puppy, who whimpered immediately.

'She's hurt.' Xander glared at Grant. 'Let me see her.'

'Oh, you want to examine her, do you? Play a vet in a film, did you?' He tugged at the lead, dragging the puppy closer to him. 'There's nothing wrong with her. She's just playing up 'cause she's got an audience.'

Rachel could feel Xander trembling with anger. It was her turn to squeeze *his* hand. 'What are you doing here, Grant? I thought you were on your way home.'

'Set off, didn't I? Got nearly all the way back to Leeds, but something kept nagging away at me. We saw you,' he said, jabbing his finger in Xander's direction. 'On the telly this afternoon. That's when Sam told me who you were.'

'What of it?' Xander enquired. Rachel peered up at him. His voice sounded suddenly different, more assured — suave, even.

'I could tell straight away that he was close to you. All that rubbish about you being away all this time! If that's true,

318

how come he was talking about you so fondly — like you were his best mate or something?'

Rachel looked up at Xander. He raised an eyebrow at her, then they both looked at Sam. He'd stopped fondling the puppy's ears and was glaring at his father, his face white with fury. ''Cause he is my best mate! He's nice to animals and doesn't hurt them, that's why. Xander wouldn't have kicked Rachel, even if she'd chewed everything he owned. He's a nice man, not like you. You're — you're horrible!'

Grant gaped at his son, clearly stunned. 'You what? How dare you speak to me like that?'

Rachel let go of Xander's hand and dashed over to Sam before Grant could do anything to him. She'd never known him hurt Sam, but she wouldn't like to take the chance that it couldn't happen. Especially seeing the look of rage on Grant's face.

Sam, however, wasn't going to go quietly. 'I want Rachel. You don't look after her. I want her to live here with me, so I can look after her.'

'Tough luck.' Grant yanked the lead again, dragging the puppy to his side, then stooped to pick her up. 'She's my dog, and if you're so ungrateful I don't see why I should give her to you. And since you clearly don't want to be around me anymore, you won't get to see her, will you? Say goodbye to the little rat.'

'No!' Sam pulled free of Rachel's grasp, ran forward and kicked his father on the shins. Grant swore and dropped the puppy on the floor, where she yelped. Grant pushed Sam out of the way and bent to pick her up again, but Xander got there first. As Rachel hurriedly dragged Sam away, Xander collected the puppy and strode over to Janie, handing her over for safekeeping.

'The puppy stays here,' he said firmly, turning to face Grant. 'You're clearly unfit to take care of her, and Sam loves her. That's the end of the matter.'

'What? Says who?' Grant seemed totally out of his depth; and, looking at this determined, sophisticated version of Xander, Rachel wasn't surprised. He was like a different man.

'Says I, my dear chap. And before you even think about starting an argument, I should point out that you would come off worse. I have had extensive training in several disciplines from the best in their field — the perks of being an actor. You're extremely lucky I don't have a sword to hand.'

Grant's mouth fell open. 'Are you having me on?'

'Certainly not. I should also remind you that you have an important job — in your eyes at least. I hardly think your clients would be impressed if you were to feature on the front pages of all the newspapers as the man who got into a fight with Lord Bay Sinclair. Believe me, the press would lap it up, and I'd be more than happy to give them all the details. After all, it's my job to court the press, and there's nothing I love more than some attention from the tabloids. If you still want to hit me, go ahead. As one of my fellow actors says — charming chap, I might add — *make my day.*'

Rachel wasn't sure who was most astonished — herself or Grant. She had never seen this side of Xander. Was this what he was like in *Lord Curtis Investigates?* No wonder he had so many fans. She didn't like the actual violence, of course, but this assured manner of his was quite a turn-on.

Grant opened his mouth to speak but didn't seem to have any words. He stared across at Sam, who was now standing pressed against Janie, one hand on the puppy's head. He looked across at Rachel, who met his gaze defiantly. Lastly, he gave Xander a filthy look, then turned and left the house, slamming the door behind him. Rachel rushed over, locked the door, then practically collapsed into Xander's arms.

'It's okay, it's okay,' he told her,

stroking her hair. He looked over at Sam. 'How's the pup?'

'She seems okay,' Janie said. 'I think she's just scared, and no wonder. I'll get her something to eat, then I'll call Merlyn. Ask him to pop over and take a look at her. He won't mind.'

'I'm sure he won't,' Rachel murmured, a smile tugging at her lips. She looked up at Xander. 'I can't believe you. You were amazing.'

Xander pulled a face. 'You didn't hear my knees knocking, clearly. I was terrified.'

'But you sounded so calm, so sure of yourself!'

'It's called acting,' he said with a grin. 'I was channelling Lord Curtis. If Grant had called my bluff I'd have been in little pieces on the floor.'

She threw her arms around his neck and giggled. 'Thank you, my brave, dashing hero. You're a star.'

'So they tell me,' he said.

She kissed him gently. 'I do love you, you know.'

'I love you, too,' he murmured. 'So much, it hurts.'

Their moment of happiness didn't last long. As a shadow passed in front of the glass panel in the door, they heard a loud thumping and the wood shook in its frame.

'He's back.' Rachel glanced across at Sam. 'Go upstairs, sweetie. Take the puppy with you.'

Sam gathered the dog in his arms, and he and Janie hurried away.

'Let me in, now!'

'I'm going to call the police,' Rachel called.

'Just give it up,' Xander shouted. 'We're not going to change our — '

There was a shattering of glass and an arm came through the broken panel. 'I said, let me in!'

'Go away,' Rachel yelled. 'I'm on the phone to the police now.'

'What's he doing?' Sam was back in the kitchen, his face showing terror.

'Sam, go upstairs!'

There was a sudden scream and

Rachel spun round, trying to take in what had happened. Outside, Grant was wailing in fright. 'Rachel, Rachel, help me! I'm dying!'

18

Xander turned off the engine and turned to look at Rachel. She took a deep breath and leaned back against the headrest. 'We're home,' he said.

'So we are.' She smiled at him. 'Thank you. For taking us, I mean. I don't think I could have managed him on my own.'

'I thought I was actually going to have to knock him out at one point, for his own safety,' Xander admitted. 'I've never seen anyone in such a state of hysteria. Although, to be fair — ' He winced. ' — it was an awful mess.'

'You're not wrong there.' Rachel shook her head. 'What an idiot, though. Bad enough that he punched through a glass window, but to then drag his arm back through it . . . No wonder he ripped himself to shreds.'

'Your poor mum, frantically swilling

the blood away, trying to keep Sam calm.'

'And the puppy paddling in it all, and nudging Grant, almost as if she were laughing at him.'

'Couldn't blame her if she was, I suppose,' Xander said. 'Ugh. It was a very nasty injury. I did wonder, at one point, if he was going to — you know — bleed to death.'

'Not with Nurse Rachel on the case.' She laughed. 'Good job Mum's so house-proud. All those clean tea towels stacked up in the airing cupboard.' She wrinkled her nose. 'Guess we'll need to buy new ones now.'

'But he will be okay?'

'Physically, yes. Not sure about his pride, though. When the doctor had calmed him down and assured him that he was going to live, didn't he look sheepish?'

'I'd like to say it serves him right, but I wouldn't wish that on anyone.' Xander cast a sly look at Rachel, who bit her lip. 'Honestly. Even him.'

'Hmm. If you say so. At least he knows where he stands now. I've got a feeling he's not going to try to bully either me or Sam again.'

'And if he wants to see Sam, he'll have to come to us and spend time at the farm with him. At least until Sam's a bit older and Grant's proved himself fit to be trusted.'

'If that ever happens. Truth is, I have a feeling that now he knows that I'm never going back, and he's lost control over both me and Sam, he'll lose interest. I just pity the next woman he gets his hooks into. Hopefully, she'll be a lot braver and wiser than I ever was.'

'You were very young, Rachel, and he caught you when you were vulnerable. You had a baby to think of, too. Don't be so hard on yourself. You're very far from a coward, and you're a hero in my book. You basically saved Grant's life.'

She laughed. 'I don't think I'd go that far, although you and Mum were surprisingly useless. She didn't know what on earth to do, and you looked as if you were going to pass out at one point.'

'Told you, I'm very different to that Curtis chap. He'd no doubt have stitched the wound himself without batting an eyelid. I need you, Rachel. I'm hopeless without you.'

Rachel tutted. 'All right, you charmer. Enough with the smooth talk. Let's go and see how Sam is, and the other Rachel.' She rolled her eyes. 'We're going to have to do something about that. Calling a dog after me. Honestly!'

Hand in hand, they strolled into the kitchen of the farmhouse, grinning at each other as they saw Janie hovering around the vet, plate of biscuits in hand.

Merlyn gave the puppy a gentle pat, then straightened. 'I don't think she's badly hurt. Maybe a bit bruised, but she's okay. She'll heal. Mind you,' he peered over his glasses at Sam, 'she's probably a bit nervous now. She's going to need lots of fuss and love and attention, young man. Are you up to the job?'

'Of course I am,' Sam said indignantly. He saw Rachel and Xander standing by the door and jumped up. 'Mum! Xander! Is Dad all right?'

'He'll be absolutely fine, Sam, don't worry.' Rachel looked over at Janie. 'They're operating on his arm tomorrow, but it should be okay.'

'I hear you were quite the heroine,' Merlyn said. 'Making a tourniquet and keeping his arm up, calming him down, issuing directions left right and centre.'

'It may have escaped your notice,' Rachel said, 'but I *am* a nurse. It would be pretty bad if I didn't know what to do.'

'You were amazing, Mum,' Sam said, admiringly. He hurried over to her and wrapped his arms around her waist. 'Totally awesome. I didn't know you could do all that. All that blood everywhere — it was proper scary — and you just sorted it out and didn't get frightened or anything. You're ever so clever.'

Rachel kissed the top of his head and glanced across at Xander, who gave her a warm smile on seeing the tears in her eyes. It seemed that Sam had finally recognised the truth about his mother, and was at last willing to give her the recognition and respect she deserved. He had a feeling Grant would never be able to exert influence over his son again.

'What a day this has been,' Janie said, placing the plate of biscuits on the table. 'I meant to tell you, Sam, Georgia called, and your next riding lesson is on Tuesday morning. You'll be able to have a lot more now it's the summer holidays.'

'I hope you don't mind,' Merlyn said, looking rather pink in the face, 'but I've asked your mother to come out for dinner with me, so I'm afraid you'll have to fend for yourselves tonight.' He hesitated, then added, rather reluctantly, 'Unless you'd all care to join us, of course.'

'I don't really want to leave Rachel,' Sam said, looking worriedly at the puppy.

'We wouldn't dream of it,' Xander said firmly. 'I'll sort our meal out. You two go and enjoy yourselves.'

'Don't tell me you can cook, too?' Rachel said, clearly impressed.

For a split second, Xander considered bluffing his way through, but realised he would soon be caught out. 'I'm a terrible cook,' he admitted. 'I'm a dab hand at ordering takeaways, though.'

'Can I go upstairs and let Rachel meet Duke and Darwin?' Sam asked.

'Of course.' Rachel put her hands on her hips. 'Before you do, though, Sam, can I ask you a favour? Would you mind if we changed her name? I really don't like having a dog named after me, even one as cute as she is.'

'I don't like it either,' Sam admitted. 'It was Dad's idea. I don't know why he chose it.'

'Well, whatever the reason,' Xander said, 'she's your dog now, and she's living here with us, so — '

'With us?' Sam's eyes widened. 'Are you living here, too, Xander?'

Xander looked at Rachel apologetically. She blushed and looked at her mother and son, an appeal in her eyes. 'Would you mind? You can say if you do.'

'Of course not!' Janie clapped her hands together in delight. 'It's wonderful, isn't it, Sam?'

'Cool,' Sam agreed. 'So, we might get a cow after all?'

'Not a chance,' Rachel laughed. 'So, a name for the puppy. What do we all think?'

'What about Smokey?' Janie suggested. 'With her being that lovely blueish colour.'

'I had a cocker spaniel once, when I was a kid,' Merlyn mused. 'Her name was Pepper.'

'We could call her Sooty,' Sam said. 'Or Peanut. Or Lucy.'

'Any ideas, Rachel?' Xander could tell she was dying to say something. She just needed a nudge.

Rachel looked around at them. 'I have got one thought,' she admitted. 'But you might think I'm being silly.'

'What is it, love?' Janie said. 'Go on. Tell us.'

'It's just that, well, this has been such a strange few months. Everything's turned around here, with all these animals getting a second chance; and you, Mum, all happy and smiling again, getting a new lease of life; and me and Sam finding a new home and starting over. Then there's Xander,' she added shyly, turning to him. 'You've finally sorted out your career, and you and I — well, you know.'

He knew. He knew all too well. His hand reached out for hers, and she smiled up at him. 'I was thinking, since Folly Farm seems to be the place for fresh starts, maybe we should call her Folly, because, after a tough beginning, she's earned her fresh start, too. What do you think?'

'Folly?' Sam considered. 'I love it! Cool. Come on, Folly. Come and meet your new friends.'

As he led her up the stairs to introduce her to Duke and Darwin, Janie turned to Merlyn. 'I'm just going to get changed. Why don't you wait in the living room?'

'What? I'm fine here, don't worry.' Xander grinned as he saw Janie shoot the vet a meaningful look, and finally it seemed to dawn on Merlyn that she was telling him to leave Rachel and Xander alone. 'Oh yes, yes, the living room. Much more comfortable.' He hurried after Janie, his face rather red.

Xander put his arms around Rachel. 'Seems like it all worked out in the end, after all.'

'It's like you told me,' she said, her eyes shining, 'everybody loves a happy ending, and it seems we've got ours at last.'

'Here's to fresh starts and happy endings,' he said.

She wrapped her arms around his neck and he bent to kiss her, knowing with absolute certainty that this truly was just the beginning of their story, and the best was yet to come.

We do hope that you have enjoyed reading this large print book.

Did you know that all of our titles are available for purchase?

We publish a wide range of high quality large print books including:
Romances, Mysteries, Classics
General Fiction
Non Fiction and Westerns

Special interest titles available in large print are:
The Little Oxford Dictionary
Music Book, Song Book
Hymn Book, Service Book

Also available from us courtesy of Oxford University Press:
Young Readers' Dictionary
(large print edition)
Young Readers' Thesaurus
(large print edition)

For further information or a free brochure, please contact us at:
Ulverscroft Large Print Books Ltd.,
The Green, Bradgate Road, Anstey,
Leicester, LE7 7FU, England.
Tel: (00 44) **0116 236 4325**
Fax: (00 44) **0116 234 0205**

COUNTRY DOCTOR

Phyllis Mallett

After years away, newly qualified Doctor Jane Ashford returns to her hometown in Essex to become a partner in her uncle's practice. Family and friends are delighted to see her again, including Steve Denny, whose crush on her has never faded. But then Jane meets local Doctor Philip Carson, both handsome and lonely; and when his touch kindles a desire that's almost painful in its intensity, she knows he's the right man for her. The problem is, Steve doesn't see it that way — and he intends to make it clear . . .

GOLDILOCKS WEDDING

Carol MacLean

Goldie Rayner wants her wedding to James to be perfect, and asks her three best friends to help. But April, Rose and Lily have their own problems: April realises that even very self-sufficient people need others sometimes, Rose must deal with the consequences of a break-in at her flat, and Lily is inundated with kittens from an unknown, and unwelcome, benefactor. And as Goldie and James find their differences rising to the surface when emotions run high, is her ex-boyfriend Bryce really the person she should be turning to?